S0-AXJ-638

The Shadow on
the Dial

The Shadow on the Dial

Anne Lindbergh

1 8 17

HARPER & ROW, PUBLISHERS

Cambridge, Philadelphia, San Francisco, Washington, London, Mexico City, São Paolo, Singapore, Sydney

NEW YORK

For Marek

The Shadow on the Dial
Copyright © 1987 by Anne S. Lindbergh
All rights reserved. No part of this book may be
used or reproduced in any manner whatsoever without
written permission except in the case of brief quotations
embodied in critical articles and reviews. Printed in
the United States of America. For information address
Harper & Row Junior Books, 10 East 53rd Street,
New York, N.Y. 10022. Published simultaneously in
Canada by Fitzhenry & Whiteside Limited, Toronto.
Designed by Joyce Hopkins
1 2 3 4 5 6 7 8 9 10
First Edition

Library of Congress Cataloging-in-Publication Data
Lindbergh, Anne.
The shadow on the dial.

Summary: Twelve-year-old Dawn and her younger
brother, Marcus, find themselves traveling to the
past and to the future when they enlist the aid of
a mysterious moving company in order to help their
crotchety great-uncle find his "heart's desire."
[1. Space and time—Fiction. 2. Uncles—Fiction.
3. Brothers and sisters—Fiction] I. Title.
PZ7.L6572Sh 1987   [Fic]   86-45783
ISBN 0-06-023882-8
ISBN 0-06-023883-6 (lib. bdg.)

"What is time? The shadow on the dial—"
—Longfellow

One

Around noon of the third day as they were passing the exit for Brunswick, Georgia, Dawn Foster accidentally on purpose dropped Luke Skywalker out the car window.

Marcus screamed.

Mrs. Foster swerved, swore, put her foot on the brake, then changed her mind and speeded up again as she noticed a trailer truck looming through the mist in the rearview mirror.

Mr. Foster jerked awake, knocking over the chocolate milk shake that Marcus had wedged between the seats at the last service area.

Mrs. Foster groped for a napkin. "What was that all about?"

1

"My milk shake!" Marcus howled. "My action figure!"

"That wasn't your milk shake," said Dawn. "It was mine."

"It was mine. You left yours on the roof of the car and it blew off. I saw it go *splat* on the highway, and a truck ran over it. I saw—"

Dawn swatted him with her activity book. "Why didn't you tell me, dummy?"

"I thought you knew," Marcus said smugly.

"That's a lie! Mom, Marcus is lying! They're going to arrest you for littering, Marcus. They'll put you in jail."

Marcus lunged and bit.

"Brat!" Dawn screamed.

"Trollop!" said Marcus.

Mrs. Foster gave him a startled look over her shoulder. Mr. Foster moaned and stretched his legs through a welter of cardboard trays and ketchup-smeared hamburger wrappings. "Don't tell me that was on your fourth-grade spelling list!"

"He said 'trollop.' Mom, he called me 'trollop.' Are you going to let him get away with it? Marcus always gets away with everything! If I called him 'trollop,' you'd stop my allowance."

Mrs. Foster groaned. "Apologize, Marcus."

"Why?" Marcus asked. "I bet she doesn't even know what it means."

"You tell me then," said Dawn. "What does it mean?"

Dawn smiled at her brother's silence. For once she had put him in his place. She had been trying to keep him in his place ever since they had left Massachusetts. And long before that too, of course, only he got on her nerves more in a cramped car than in a big house in the country. The problem was, he wouldn't *stay* in his place. He kept popping right up again, doing something bratty, saying some-

2

thing silly, and getting all the attention just the same. It used to be Dawn who got the attention. Her teachers said she was promising. Especially her music teachers: talented, they said. Her parents had acted proud. But lately they seemed to ignore her talents and notice only Marcus.

Dawn sank back into the daydreams that had lulled her through the long drive from Massachusetts. In them she was driving too.

Driving south in a shiny limousine with tinted windows, so she could see out but nobody could see in. Because famous people didn't like ordinary people staring in. There was a window inside the limousine too, dividing the backseat from the front so no one could bother her, and there was a bar with soft drinks and a T.V.

She was alone. No, Marcus was with her, because he had promised to keep quiet if she let him come for a ride. He was grateful: She had never allowed him to come before. She made two chocolate milk shakes and gave him one.

"You make delicious milk shakes," Marcus said humbly.

"Really? Usually my chauffeur makes them, but he's busy driving now."

"May I watch *Star Trek* on your T.V.?" Marcus asked.

"I'm afraid not. I need to watch a replay of my performance on the Johnny Carson show."

Sipping her chocolate milk shake, Dawn sat back and watched herself on T.V.

She wore black: a long black dress, off the shoulders, so simple that you couldn't get away with it unless you had a perfect figure. But people hardly noticed the dress, because Dawn was playing such heavenly music.

"That was Dawn Foster, the girl with the singing flute!"

3

Johnny Carson said when the last notes died away. "Dawn has won every award there is to win in the United States, and we're proud to have her with us tonight. Tell us, Dawn Foster, what are your plans for the future?"

Dawn answered in a voice as lovely as the music she had played: "From now on, I plan to devote my life to ballet. I am also a famous ballerina."

"You're the wrong shape for a ballerina," Marcus said. "Ballerinas are skinny."

Dawn jumped in her seat. Was he a mind reader, or had she really spoken aloud? "That's an optical illusion," she informed her brother. "They just look skinny onstage. Besides, who said anything about ballerinas?"

"You did."

Dawn blushed. "You're crazy. I'm going to be a flutist— I already told you that."

"You're not going to be anything at all unless you practice," her mother remarked. "Serious musicians practice five or six hours a day, you know. Your flute teacher is lucky if he gets one hour a week out of you."

Dawn glared at the back of her head. "That's because I have to do my barre exercises."

"Another hour a week," said Mrs. Foster. "Face it, Dawnie. If you want to get something, you have to give something."

Dawn glared harder. "I'm musical, right? My problem is that I have too many choices."

"Well, watch it," her mother said. "Before you know it, you'll grow up, and it'll be too late. Musicians have to start early."

Dawn exploded. "Preach, preach, preach! Why don't you ever preach at Marcus for a change?"

"Because I'm not musical," Marcus said contentedly.

4

With the only fingernail she hadn't gnawed down to the quick, Dawn reinforced the toothmarks on her arm. If she kept jabbing all the way to Sunset Grove, with luck the wound would be bad enough to get Marcus into trouble. It might even bleed.

"Are we there yet?" she asked.

"We're still in Georgia," her father reminded her wearily. "After we cross the state line, we take Route Four across Florida to the Gulf coast. Then it's south sixty miles to Sunset Grove. We won't be there until this evening. Got that?"

Dawn reached out her arms. Moving toward the front of the stage in her long white nightgown on bare feet, she was the most graceful Clara in the history of *The Nutcracker*. She was young, innocent, unpretentious. Every performance had been sold out, but she had managed to get her parents two seats in the front row. They sat staring up at her with pride on their faces, tears in their eyes—

"This weather is unbelievable!" Mrs. Foster switched on the windshield wipers and frowned at the highway stretching slickly before her.

"Let Dad drive," Dawn said. "You've been passing that same truck ever since South Carolina, and then you let him pass *you* again, and if I smell any more truck pollution I'm going to throw up all over Marcus."

Marcus inched away from her. "Which truck? Allied Vans?"

"The one without any license plates."

"It couldn't not have any license plates," Marcus said. "If a truck doesn't have a license plate it gets arrested. Most of them have *lots* of license plates."

5

"That's why I noticed, dummy. It's the one with the bald-headed driver."

"Oh, you mean Bros Removers." Marcus recited in a singsong voice: " '20th Century Bros Removers. Est 1901. Your Heart's Desire. Just Dial.' What's a bros remover, Mom? What's 'Est'?"

"Abbreviations," Mrs. Foster explained. " 'Est' means established, Marcus. 'Bros' is short for brothers. And it must be 'movers,' not removers. Besides, just dial what?"

Marcus shrugged. "It didn't say."

"He made the whole thing up," said Dawn. "Didn't he, Dad?"

Mr. Foster settled back in his seat and shut his eyes. "Ask your mother."

"No way!" Mrs. Foster told her husband firmly. "I'm driving. When you drive, I cope; when I drive, you cope. That was the deal, so sit up and cope."

Mr. Foster sat up. "Okay, kids. We'll let them pass us again and see who's right."

"I warn you, I'll throw up," said Dawn.

Her mother took her foot off the pedal while the van pulled out into the passing lane and thundered by.

"See?" Marcus pointed triumphantly at the large black letters:

20th CENTURY
BROS REMOVERS
EST 1901
Your
Heart's
Desire
JUST DIAL

Mr. Foster laughed. " 'Heart's Desire'? How corny can you get! And I can't believe the guy has no license plates.

State troopers usually spot that kind of thing in a flash. Pass him again, Liz."

Mrs. Foster accelerated.

"Weird-looking character," Mr. Foster commented, peering up at the driver. "Bald as a baby. And you're right, it doesn't say what number to dial. How about it, Dawnie—convinced?"

Startled by sudden silence in the backseat, he twisted around to see what was the matter. Marcus had shrunk into his corner, putting as much space as possible between himself and his sister, whose face had turned an ashy gray.

"Truck pollution," Dawn whispered, and she cupped her hand over her mouth.

"There's a roadside rest area ahead, Liz," Mr. Foster said. "We'll stretch our legs."

Marcus whined, "Not a rest area—please Dad, not a rest area! There's a service area in nineteen miles, the sign said. I need another milk shake."

"I don't think Dawn can hold out for nineteen miles. Anyway, it's my turn to drive." Straining his seat belt, Mr. Foster leaned forward to gather the trash from around his ankles.

"How much farther do you have to drive after you leave me and Dawn with Mr. Doolittle?" Marcus asked as the car turned into the ramp.

"Uncle Doo," said his mother. "He wants you to call him Uncle Doo."

"Why? He's your uncle, not mine."

"If you call him Great-Uncle Doo, you'll make him feel old."

"But he *is* old," said Marcus. "He's eighty-one. How much older can you get?"

"Uncle Doo will live to be a hundred if you two don't wear him out this week."

7

Dawn uncovered her mouth long enough to whimper, "I don't want to stay with an old man in Sunset Grove. I'd rather go with you two to Key West. Why are you trying to get rid of us?"

"Your mother and I haven't had a week by ourselves for years," Mr. Foster said sharply. "We're going, and we'll join you on Christmas Eve, and that's that. Most kids would give their eyeteeth to be staying in Sunset Grove."

"Besides, you're going to love it." Mrs. Foster made her voice sound soothing. "The beach is gorgeous and my uncle Doo is an old sweetie. He was my favorite uncle when I was your age."

"And now?" Marcus asked. "Is he still your favorite uncle?"

"Well . . ." Mrs. Foster sighed. "Back then I adored him. I thought he could do just about anything. But it turned out he never did much at all. He just wandered from one job to another, and now he's old. That makes me feel a little sad."

"What about him?" Dawn asked. "Is he sad too?"

Mrs. Foster shook her head and smiled. "Actually, he seems perfectly content with life."

"Then why don't you leave him alone?" Dawn demanded. "It's just like with me: push, push, preach, preach. Why don't you leave both of us alone?"

"Think about it," Mrs. Foster said.

Dawn thought about it and sympathized with Uncle Doo, even though she hadn't met him. They were both people who wanted to lead their own lives, make their own decisions, without any bossing around. "Maybe I don't mind staying with him after all," she said.

Mrs. Foster turned off the engine and climbed wearily out of the driver's seat. "Out you get, Dawn. A little fresh air will make you feel a whole lot better."

8

Dawn slumped down in the backseat. "No thanks. I don't feel sick anymore. And you'd better pull your tail in, Mom, or Bros Removers will remove it. He's heading straight for us, and I don't think he read that sign about the twenty-five-mph ramp speed."

Mrs. Foster flattened herself against the car. "Stay away from that maniac!" she called to Marcus, who had run toward the van for a closer look. "Maybe we'd better get a head start, come to think of it. I'm tired of playing cat and mouse with him."

Marcus strolled back with an angelic expression on his face and climbed into the car. Dawn's eyes were shut, but he prodded her with a folded sheet of paper.

"Look what I got!" he whispered. "It's some kind of a coupon. See? 'One Heart's Desire, deliverable upon demand.' "

Dawn's eyes popped open. "Did the driver give it to you?"

"Are you kidding? I snitched it when he was in the Jiffy-John."

Dawn studied the coupon carefully. "You shouldn't have taken it. It says, 'Not transferable. Valid when endorsed by lawful owner only.' You're not the owner."

"Well, I am now." Marcus took a ballpoint pen and wrote his name boldly across the line provided for a signature: "Marcus Foster."

"That doesn't make you the *lawful* owner. I bet he follows us and wants it back. I bet you're in real trouble, Marcus."

She looked over her shoulder as they pulled back onto the highway. The bald-headed truck driver had returned to his van and it was moving up the ramp behind them.

9

Two

Uncle Doo's living room felt like an outdoor porch on a damp day. It was sodden with the kind of chill Dawn expected back home in Massachusetts, but not in Florida. She hugged her bare arms around her bare knees and prayed for Uncle Doo to turn on the furnace.

Uncle Doo did not look like an old sweetie. Dawn couldn't imagine him as anybody's favorite uncle. He was bony and private faced. Two deep lines between his brows showed that he spent more time frowning than smiling. His clothes were old and rather loose on him, but they were spotlessly clean and newly ironed. He knelt with his back to them, across the room, sponging the plastic mat

10

he kept at the front door. As if they were the first children in the history of the world to leave dirt on a doormat, Dawn thought.

She turned to Marcus, who sat next to her on the sofa. "See the thermostat on the wall over there? Go turn it up!"

"You do it," Marcus said. "I'm too cold."

He moved closer, but Dawn moved too. She needed the warmth, but she couldn't take the smell: Marcus, not Dawn, had been sick in the car.

"You stink," she said. "You need a bath."

Marcus reached for a cushion and pressed it to his chest. Absentmindedly, he plucked at a loop in the cloth.

Uncle Doo gave the doormat one last dab and stood up. "Don't!"

Marcus jumped. "Don't what?"

"Don't fool with that cushion. Just had the sofa re-covered. That cloth gadget on the floor fits over the arm, to keep it clean. Put it back on."

Marcus reached for the cloth and slipped it back into place. "I don't like it here," he said under his breath. "Where do you think Mom and Dad are now?"

Dawn studied her wristwatch. "They've been gone for exactly seventeen minutes. They're probably still in the suburbs of Sunset Grove."

"This whole place is a suburb," Marcus said. "I hate suburbs."

"We live in the suburbs of Boston and you like it there," Dawn reminded him.

"No I don't. Just because you're older doesn't mean you can say what I like and don't like."

Dawn tuned him out. Shutting her eyes, she refurnished the room, giving the windows golden drapes, the floor a

11

soft, white rug made of real fur. She added a fireplace with a roaring fire. She added Dawn Foster, curled up on the sofa in a sexy silk bathrobe, watching herself on T.V.

Johnny Carson held up his hands in horror. "But Ms. Foster, you can't do that. You haven't the right! An artist of your caliber hasn't the right to make such a decision. Your gift no longer belongs to you, if you'll forgive my saying so. It belongs to the public. Please say you'll change your mind!"

"Well, maybe you're right," Dawn Foster said, and she lifted the singing flute to her mouth, unable to stop the applause of the studio audience, forced to play an encore—

The phone rang. Dawn Foster reached for it lazily. "Could you call back later?" she asked. "I'm on T.V. right now."

"This is your mother," said the caller. "Why didn't you tell me you were on T.V.?"

"I'm on T.V. so often that I hardly notice anymore," said Dawn. "It's such a bore!"

"It's never a bore to *me,* dear," her mother said. "I'll call you back after the show is over."

"I may be out," said Dawn.

"I don't want to go out," Marcus grumbled. "It's raining, and I'm cold. I wish we could go back home."

Dawn opened her eyes and made a dizzying effort to focus on the present. Her brother's words hung inside her head for a moment before they made sense.

"I do too," she said. "Not drive back, just *be* back."

"If we dial, maybe Bros Removers would remove us there. I've still got the coupon." Marcus fished in his pocket and read aloud: " 'One Heart's Desire, deliverable upon demand. Just Dial. Expiration date December 31, 1999.' "

"Who wants to wait until then?" Dawn asked. "I can

think of a lot of things I want right now. Like being back home, or down in Key West with Mom and Dad."

Marcus shivered. "I'd settle for being warm—right here, right now."

"Then turn up the thermostat."

"You do."

Dawn sighed. They were back where they had started. "I'd better ask him first. The thing is, I don't know what to call him. 'Uncle Doo' doesn't seem respectful."

"So far, I say 'you,' " Marcus said.

"We can't say 'Hey, you!' for a whole week," Dawn objected.

"I think I'll put on more clothes." Stiffly, Marcus lowered his feet, rose from the sofa, shuffled toward the room he was to share with his sister.

Dawn hugged her knees tighter. Was she cold enough to get some jeans and a sweatshirt out of her suitcase? No, she'd just grow colder and colder until she turned blue. She might even catch pneumonia—pneumonia in Florida! Then her parents would be sorry they'd left her behind with Marcus and Uncle Doo.

Why hadn't they let her go along to Key West? She wouldn't have been in the way. She would have practiced flute, practiced her barre exercises, and kept out of sight, if that was what they wanted. But she knew that if they had taken anyone along, it would have been Marcus. Because he was the youngest. What was the good of being the oldest? She got all the preaching, that was all, while Marcus got spoiled.

Outside, rain rattled in the palmetto spikes, streaked down the concrete drive, bruised the gaudy, purple blossoms that didn't grow in Massachusetts. Because of rain, the same old rain that fell back home, she was trapped in Uncle Doo's living room.

13

Looking around her, Dawn thought that Uncle Doo's living room was like a display in a furniture store. Everything glittered with a fake, frosty light: the drapes, the carpet, the protective cellophane that Uncle Doo had never removed from his lampshades, and the wallpaper that looked like Christmas wrapping.

She scraped lightly at the wallpaper with her one good fingernail. Uncle Doo, appearing suddenly before her, said, "Don't!"

"Have you lived in this same place the whole time you've been in Sunset Grove?" Dawn asked. "Everything looks new."

"Let's try and keep it that way," said Uncle Doo. "Thirteen years, and I haven't been obliged to replace a thing. Had the sofa recovered, is all, and had the rug cleaned once. That was due to flooding from the hurricane, back in seventy-eight."

Uncle Doo's apartment was part of a condominium called Sunset Arcade, a ten-story rectangle striped with balconies overlooking Sunset Beach. Uncle Doo's balcony was the only one with no view of the beach. All Dawn could see from it was the mess of pumps behind a heated swimming pool. This was because instead of being attached to the main building, the apartment stood by itself at the edge of the parking lot, like a service station. It had been built as a model and would have been torn down, except that Uncle Doo had taken a liking to the place. Not only was it private, he had explained to the children: Thirteen years ago he had bought it dirt cheap.

It might have been cheap, but it was anything but private, Dawn thought. Cars kept pulling up to within a few feet of their windows on three sides. On the swimming-pool side some men were repairing the pipes. Dawn parted

14

the filmy rayon drapes but let them fall into place again when the men turned to stare at her.

"This is kind of like living in a zoo," she said.

Uncle Doo gave her an inquiring glance.

"Not because it stinks or anything," she added quickly, "but don't you feel like everything you do is kind of public?"

"No," said Uncle Doo.

Dawn changed the subject. "Can we swim in the pool?"

"It's raining."

"That's okay," Dawn said. "We'd get wet anyway."

"Sorry. There's a rule: No children under twelve unless accompanied by an adult."

"I'm not under twelve, I'm three months *over* twelve."

"It's too late. Suppertime."

"But I'm not hungry!" Dawn protested. "Marcus can't eat anything either. He got sick in the car."

Marcus reappeared, in long pants and a sweater. Dawn noticed that he wore two pairs of socks, making his shoes bulge as if his feet were swollen.

"I'm not hungry and I'm not swimmy, either," he announced. "I'm cold." Drawing his feet up under him, he curled into a corner of the sofa.

"Don't!" said Uncle Doo.

"Don't what?"

"Don't put your shoes on the sofa. Look at them— covered with sand!"

Marcus looked down at his shoes, looked up at Uncle Doo again, shrugged, and left the room. Dawn heard the bedroom door shut behind him: not the rebellious slam she might have heard at home, just a quiet little click. Something boiled inside her.

"Did you know you were my mother's favorite uncle?" she asked.

15

Uncle Doo raised his eyebrows. "I am?"

"Were. You *were* my mother's favorite uncle. I guess you must have been really nice to kids. Back then."

Uncle Doo froze for a moment. He stared at Dawn as if he were wishing her out of the house. Then the stare softened and a smile flicked tentatively across his face.

"I've been looking forward," he said gruffly. "Got to set some rules, though, right from the start. No food in the living room, for one thing. No wet bathing suits, ever. Hose your feet off—we don't want half of Sunset Beach in here. No shouting, or we'll get complaints. Average age in this place is a hundred and two, in case you haven't noticed. No shells and that sort of thing—"

"How about no kids?" Dawn suggested angrily.

But Uncle Doo said, "About time I had children in the house." He turned his back and walked into the kitchen.

"I don't know why we call him Uncle Doo," Marcus muttered as he toyed with his frozen fish sticks at supper. "His name ought to be 'Uncle Don't!' "

"Better not let him hear you call him that."

"He can't hear. He's making too much clatter." Marcus glanced over his shoulder toward the sink, where Uncle Doo was washing dishes. "I don't like this place, Dawnie. Do you?"

A sour knot of homesickness tightened in Dawn's stomach. "It's got that pool," she said, more to convince herself than to cheer Marcus. "It's got T.V."

"There's nothing but news on T.V.," Marcus said, "and the pool looks closed. There's this big plastic cover over it, and a whole heap of dead roaches and stuff on top."

It was growing dark. The cars that drew up to the windows had their headlights on now, and Dawn wondered how much was visible through Uncle Doo's flimsy curtains. Could people see the T.V., where the news commentator had been yapping noiselessly since Marcus turned the volume down? Could they see Uncle Doo in the kitchenette? Could they see Marcus rubbing the side of his nose—ready to pick it, Dawn guessed, the minute she looked away?

"Don't pick your nose—it's gross," she said in a fair imitation of her mother. Then her voice changed. "Hey, Marcus! He's got a piano. Do you think he'd mind if I played?"

"Probably," said Marcus, and his eyes retreated to the T.V. screen.

Back home in Massachusetts, the Fosters had a big mahogany upright with old-fashioned carving that made Dawn think of church windows. The top seven keys played the same note, and the bottom four didn't play at all. It had cost fifty dollars at a yard sale. But Uncle Doo's piano was in keeping with the rest of his furniture: trim and tidy, and lacquered white. It was perfectly tuned. For once, Dawn thought, "Chopsticks" sounded good.

Marcus switched off the T.V. and ran across the room. "I'll play the top part!"

"Oh, no you won't!"

Marcus played, missing most of the notes and pinching his sister's wrist whenever her right hand trespassed above middle C.

"Quit that, you little brat! I was here first."

"That's why it's my turn now."

"You don't get a turn. You don't take lessons. Playing piano is supposed to help me with the flute. My teacher said."

17

"You made that up!"

A long, bony arm reached between them and shut the lid. "Fun's over," said Uncle Doo. "Time to get ready."

"Ready for what?" If they had been at home, they would have been putting away their homework and getting ready for bed.

"Friday-night concert at the church," said Uncle Doo.

"Church music?" Marcus asked suspiciously.

"Real music. Good music." This time, Uncle Doo's smile was successful. "Haven't missed a Friday-night concert in thirteen years."

Dawn thought for a moment. "Not even for the hurricane?"

"The hurricane was on a Tuesday," said Uncle Doo. "We're leaving in five minutes, soon as I change into my church togs."

Dawn went back to the T.V. and found an old black-and-white movie where the women wore their kinky hair plastered close to their heads like bathing caps. She was already so close to laughing that when she saw Uncle Doo in his church togs, she couldn't keep back a giggle. He had changed into emerald-green slacks, a shirt with a pattern of interlocking pink flamingos, and a somber, pin-striped jacket that looked like the top half of a suit. It struck Dawn that Uncle Doo must have lost a lot of weight since he had bought that jacket. He was a lean man, and the jacket had been cut for a bulging stomach.

Uncle Doo heard the giggle and looked shyer than ever. Dawn wished she had kept quiet. "Better move it," she called to Marcus, "or Uncle Don't will be late for his concert!"

Realizing what she had said, she turned red and rushed blindly toward the closest door.

18

"DON'T!" shouted Uncle Doo.

Dawn froze in her steps. What had she done wrong this time?

"Sorry," Uncle Doo said. "I just meant don't fool with that door. It doesn't go anywhere."

"How can a door not go anywhere?" Marcus asked. "It has to—otherwise it wouldn't be there."

"Ordinarily, yes," Uncle Doo agreed. "In the condo apartments that door would lead to the elevator. This place hasn't got an elevator."

Dawn looked around the room, taking her bearings. "It goes to the south side of the parking lot," she calculated.

"It doesn't go anywhere," Uncle Doo repeated firmly. "I've got a bit of a garden back there, that's all. If you went out that door, you'd step right into my dahlias."

On the way to the car, Dawn looked for Uncle Doo's garden. She didn't believe there was room for one, but she was wrong. A narrow strip of lawn separated the house from the parking lot. In the near dark, she could make out flowers, a small bench, and a sundial.

"That's pretty!" she said. "You're a good gardener."

"Thanks," said Uncle Doo. "Not much space to work with, but I made the best of what there was. Sometimes I think it's the only work I ever did that came to anything."

"What work *did* you do?" Dawn asked.

"Oh, a little of this and a little of that. Jack of all trades, you might call me. Started out thinking I was good at a bunch of things, and never could choose."

"That's like me," said Dawn.

"No, it's not. You're young. You can get what you want out of life. Only thing is, if you get something, you have to give something too. But no use telling you that, I suppose. Pearls before swine."

19

Dawn groaned. "Why does everybody preach at me? I hate preaching!"

Uncle Doo caught his breath. Then he chuckled. "A little preaching won't hurt you. That's what my father used to say."

There was something odd about his voice. Dawn turned to look at him and saw such a bitter expression on his face that she was frightened.

"Uncle Doo, are you okay?"

"We'll be late," Uncle Doo announced, his face suddenly expressionless again. He took her by the elbow and steered her to the car.

Marcus was already in the back seat, looking lost. Dawn knew why. Although not a chauffeured limousine, Uncle Doo's car was long, low, and shiny. When Uncle Doo pressed a button on the dashboard, the windows closed silently, shutting out the wet, fragrant Florida night and leaving only the smell of new upholstery. No one had ever spilled a milk shake or been carsick in this car. Dawn thought of her parents' battered station wagon, and the knot in her stomach became tighter still.

The Church of Our Savior of Sunset Grove was unlike any church in Massachusetts. Its white stucco walls were flanked by flowering shrubs: waxy camellias, flaming red hibiscus, and hothouse blooms that would never have survived outdoors in New England. Dawn wouldn't have guessed it was a church at all if it hadn't been for a neon sign out on the lawn. It flashed two messages alternately: first JESUS LOVES YOU, then WEAR A SMILE—ONE SIZE FITS ALL. Everyone inside was wearing a smile, and all the men wore brightly patterned shirts like Uncle Doo's.

Pews had been arranged in a semicircle around one music stand and a piano. Dawn was relieved to see that not everyone was a hundred and two: Sitting in a front pew were two girls, one about her age and one a little younger.

"There's room next to those children," Uncle Doo whispered, giving Dawn and Marcus a little push. "They're from the condominium. I'll introduce you later."

The lights were dimmed as soon as they sat down, barely leaving time to learn from the program that Sarah Sneed and Anna Purvis would perform music by Bartók, Bach, and Grieg. Then two women—one plump and one narrow, but both wearing apricot chiffon—walked in and bowed. The plump one sat down on the piano bench, bouncing gently as she worried the knobs that made it higher or lower, while the other tucked a violin under a sharp chin and plucked at the strings. The audience stopped talking. For a moment the only sound was the patter of rain against the stained-glass windows.

As far as Dawn and Marcus were concerned, they would rather hear rain than Bartók. They listened for thirty seconds before relaxing into the dazed stupor that is the polite alternative to fidgeting. The two girls from the condominium did the same, coming to life only when grown-ups around them started clapping. Marcus clapped too, but Dawn was in a different theater.

Dressed in a tutu as crisp and ragged as a white carnation, she was the second of three cygnets. Each step precise, each gesture synchronized, she moved in perfect harmony with the dancers on either side. But the audience knew she was the best. There wasn't a doubt in their minds that when Dawn Foster had grown a little older, a little more experienced, she would dance Odette in the most thrilling performance in the history of *Swan Lake*.

The applause was deafening. Her parents and Marcus,

21

in the first row, rose to a standing ovation, and the rest of the audience rose with them, clapping until their hands—

"Why don't you clap?" Marcus asked. "It's rude not to clap, especially up front where they can see you."

"I'll clap when I feel like it," Dawn whispered. But she forced herself to listen to the music.

The next piece was by Bach. The violinist played it alone. She played dramatically: swaying, flourishing her bow, wincing from time to time as if the music hurt. There were several parts, and after each part Dawn and Marcus clapped. No one else applauded, but Dawn was so determined to outclap Marcus that she didn't notice.

"You shouldn't have done that," one of the girls from the condominium told them when the piece was over. "You're supposed to wait until the very end."

Marcus's face clouded. "Why didn't you warn us?"

"We thought you knew," the other girl said. "Everybody knows that."

Dawn instantly hated both girls and was annoyed when Uncle Doo came to introduce them in the intermission.

"This is Kelly," he said, nodding at one, "and this is her sister Lisa. You'll be seeing a lot of each other."

"They were clapping between movements, Mr. Doolittle," Kelly informed him in a sugary voice. "It was really embarrassing. I think you should explain to them what's good manners at concerts."

Dawn cringed with shame and anger. She didn't dare look Uncle Doo in the face, and was astonished at his reply.

"Dawn happens to dislike preaching," he said crisply. "Can't say that I blame her. Mind your own manners, and don't concern yourself with hers."

22

Kelly grabbed Lisa's hand and headed for the refreshment table.

"Thanks, Uncle Doo!" Dawn said. "Do we really have to see a lot of them?"

"That's up to you. And no more clapping between movements. Haven't you had any musical education?"

"Of course we have," Dawn told him indignantly. "Marcus is in the church choir back home, and I play the flute."

Uncle Doo's jaw dropped. "Flute? You're a flutist?"

Dawn nodded.

"Wonders never cease!" Uncle Doo's face was bitter for the second time that evening. "I always wished I played the flute myself. Did you bring your instrument?"

"She left it in the car," Marcus informed him. "I saw her shove it under the seat, so she wouldn't have to practice on vacation. It'll probably get stolen, and it's really valuable. Mom says it belonged to her great-uncle Arthur, and it's been in the family for close to a century."

"Tattletale!" said Dawn.

Uncle Doo stopped smiling. "Well, run along and get some punch and cookies, and remember—if you aren't sure when to applaud, wait for the rest of the audience."

"He's mean!" said Marcus, watching him walk away.

Dawn shook her head; she remembered the bitter face. It had looked as if Uncle Doo was mad at someone, and she didn't think it was her and Marcus. Where was the Uncle Doo her mother had adored? Had he been preached at too much, just like Dawn? Dawn promised herself to find the old Uncle Doo and bring him back to life. After all, if there were two in her family who felt the same, they should stick together.

"Let's skip the punch and cookies," she said. "We might meet those girls again. I wish we'd stayed home tonight."

"I could have been watching *Star Trek*—" Marcus stopped suddenly and grabbed his sister's sleeve. "Look!"

Dawn gasped. A few feet away, staring at her and Marcus, was the bald-headed truck driver who had kept pace with them all the way from South Carolina. She hadn't noticed his face then, but now it astonished her. It was cold and uncompromising, and his eyes were like flashlights aimed blindingly at her on a dark night.

Her instinct was to turn and slip into the crowd, but she found that she couldn't budge. "What are you doing here?" She tried to sound normal, but her voice sharpened to a squeak.

The man smiled cynically. "Listening to music."

"So are we." Marcus glanced desperately over his shoulder. "Dawn, let's go back and sit down."

"One moment, please." The man's words were pleasant, but Dawn felt the shadow of a threat in his voice. "A moment of your precious time. There's a little matter of a coupon."

"Coupon?" Dawn forgot to shut her mouth after she spoke.

"*He* has it." The man nodded at Marcus. "He's not the lawful owner, but I won't dispute that point. An hour or so ago he mentioned dialing. His exact words, if I'm not mistaken, were 'If we dial, maybe Bros Removers would remove us there.' "

Marcus laughed nervously. "How do you know?"

The man crossed his arms.

"Well, maybe he did," said Dawn, "but it was just a manner of speaking."

"I wouldn't presume to discuss your manners," the man said. "The point is, are you interested in one-way or round trip?"

24

Dawn nibbled on her last good fingernail. This was crazy! If her friends back home were there, they would laugh and run away, and she would run with them. But something deep inside told her this was important. As important as the bitter look on Uncle Doo's face, and just as real. Besides, she couldn't even move, not to speak of run. Marcus looked paralyzed as well. What was going on?

When her silence became embarrassing, she decided to play along. After all, there were plenty of people to come to her rescue. "One-way to where?" she asked.

"To Heart's Desire. Where else?"

"Is that a place?" Marcus opened his eyes wide.

The man shrugged impatiently. "For some it's a place, for others it's a person or a thing. Haven't you a Heart's Desire? If not, why did you take the coupon? I'm afraid you're wasting my time."

"Heart's Desire!" Marcus gave a little jump. "Could I get Luke Skywalker back? Or even have a complete set of *Star Wars* action figures?"

Dawn found that her feet could move now too, but she no longer tried to run away. "Anything I want? You mean I could go to Heart's Desire, and when I came back I'd be a famous ballerina?"

The man wagged a finger at her. "A ballerina, yes. Come back, no. Your own Heart's Desire is one-way, remember."

Dawn stamped her foot. In her excitement she had completely forgotten to be afraid. "I can't remember something I never knew in the first place. How do you get a round trip, then?"

"Only if it's someone else's Heart's Desire."

Dawn thought hard. "I know! I'll wish the action figures for Marcus, and Marcus can wish something for me."

The man's scorn was so obvious that her knees trembled. He turned away.

"Wait, don't go!" Dawn cried. "We'll think of something, I promise. And we want round trip. But how do we do it?"

"Just dial. Then wait for the van."

The man moved toward the exit, but before he could leave, the plump pianist ran over and tugged at his sleeve.

"Mr. Bros! I thought I'd never see you again! But why are you leaving?"

Mr. Bros slowed down. "Sorry, my dear. 'Music hath charms to soothe the savage breast,' but my work involves the happiness of others, as you well know."

"As I well know," Miss Purvis repeated, "and a lot of good it ever did me."

Suddenly she turned to stare at Dawn and Marcus. "You two, back again! I never thought I'd see you either. What are you doing here?"

"I don't think we've met before," Dawn said timidly. "We came with Mr. Doolittle. He's our great-uncle."

Miss Purvis stared a moment longer. Then she shook her head confusedly. "It isn't fair. I'm an old woman now, and all I want is peace."

Dawn watched her walk away and took a deep breath. "They're both crazy. Completely bonkers. It was all I could do not to laugh."

"Me too," said Marcus.

But his face was troubled, and secretly Dawn didn't feel like laughing either.

Three

The sky was overcast, although the rain had stopped. Marcus dressed quickly and stood gazing out the window while Dawn tried on several outfits before deciding on the shorts and shirt she had worn the day before.

"It doesn't look too warm out there," Marcus warned her. "People are wearing sweaters."

Dawn peered over his shoulder. "Only little old ladies. Little old ladies always wear sweaters, even on the equator. White orlon sweaters, with pearl collars. Look—Uncle Doo's car is gone!"

"He's at the library," Marcus informed her. "He helps out three mornings a week. I heard him talking about it with the fat lady in the orange dress."

"Not orange, apricot," said Dawn. "And she wasn't what I'd call fat. Just a little dumpy. I thought she was more attractive than the skinny one with the violin."

"You would," Marcus said, looking her up and down.

"Oh, don't be so smart-alecky. I don't mean her shape. She's got pretty hair, like someone a lot younger. It's real, and there's plenty of it. Not like the kind of old lady who dyes it blue and gets it all kinked up at the hairdresser's. Didn't you notice?"

"No," said Marcus.

"Well, you must have noticed her face, anyway. She really looks at you, kind of like she's asking you a question. Usually only dogs look at you that way."

Marcus burst out laughing. "I'll tell her that. I'll say, 'You know what? Dawn thinks you look like a dog.'"

"Go ahead, if you dare." Dawn sat down at the dining-room table where Uncle Doo had set two places and put out a box of Grape-Nuts and some bananas. She was slicing a banana into her cereal when Marcus came back carrying a tray. Dawn stared. It was loaded with a bowl of lemon sherbet, a glass of Coke, seven pretzels, and a slice of liverwurst.

"You can't eat that for breakfast!"

"Oh, can't I?" Marcus spread liverwurst on a pretzel and spooned a dollop of sherbet on top.

"Gross!" said Dawn. "Can I try?"

She nibbled, keeping the food well to the front of her mouth and avoiding Marcus's eyes.

Marcus was the first to give up. "Gross," he agreed, spitting it into his cereal bowl. He looked reproachfully at the cereal, carried the bowl to the kitchenette, and scraped it into the garbage disposal.

"Who needs breakfast?" he said. "Let's go to the beach."

28

To get to the beach they made a wide detour around the condominium, weaving between parked cars, then following concrete paths that looked safe but were scattered with tiny sand burrs. Marcus wasn't wearing shoes. He had to stop several times along the way to wrench the burrs from the soles of his feet: a painful business since each burr was barbed. Dawn knew he was in a mood to pick a fight.

"You sure looked silly last night while that Mr. Bros was talking to you," he said out of the blue.

"Speak for yourself," Dawn replied automatically. She had just spotted Kelly and Lisa outside a video arcade, a hundred yards away. "There are those creeps we met at the concert. Let's go in the other direction."

It was too late. The two sisters stared, then walked toward them.

"There's nothing to do in this dump, is there!" Kelly said. "They won't open the pool. They say it's too cold. Want a game of Donkey Kong?"

"Who's paying?" Marcus asked.

"You pay for yours, we'll pay for ours."

Dawn shook her head. "We don't have any money."

"Why don't you ask Mr. Doolittle?"

Dawn shrugged, put her hands in her pockets, kicked at the sand. "Come on, Marcus."

Leaving the sisters, they went to the water's edge. The beach was deserted now, except for an old man in white net shoes who combed the tide line for last night's shells.

"Do you suppose we ought to have gone with them?" Dawn asked.

"No," Marcus said. "I'd rather be with you."

She glanced suspiciously at him. "What did you mean when you said I looked silly last night?"

29

"Scared silly. Scared stiff."

Dawn glared. "Who's the one who was so scared he couldn't budge, with his mouth wide open like a baby?"

"You," said Marcus.

Dawn ignored him. "Do you think he was kidding?" she asked.

"I think he was crazy."

"Miss Purvis wouldn't have talked to him like that if he were crazy," she objected.

"Who's Miss Purvis?"

"Oh, you know, the dumpy one you were talking about, who played the piano. She kind of respected him—I could tell."

"How come they knew each other?" Marcus wondered. "A piano lady and a truck driver? That's weird!"

They walked on, passing two more beach-front condominiums and a Holiday Inn. There were lounging chairs for rent in front of the motel. A few vacationers lay on them, glistening with suntan oil. Dawn felt sorry for them; they were rigid with cold.

"Are they out of their minds?" Marcus said. "There's no sun!"

"They're out for their money's worth," Dawn said. "Maybe they're just here for the weekend, and it's been raining the whole time. Anyway, remember Dad said you could get a burn even when the sky is overcast?"

"Sure," Marcus said scornfully. "Plus pneumonia. I bet they wish *they* could dial Bros Removers and get removed."

Dawn shivered. She looked down at her bare legs and noticed goose bumps. She wasn't sure they were from the cold. "I won't do it!" she announced.

Marcus stared. "Won't do what?"

"That Heart's Desire business. It's some kind of trick."

30

Marcus walked a few inches into the water. Each time the ripples swept around his feet and withdrew, his feet sank farther into the sand. "Quicksand," he said.

"Quicksand is mud. You'd be dead by now."

"I want to try." Marcus waded out.

Dawn knew he was not referring to death by quicksand. "It can't be real," she said, "and even if it's real, it's dangerous. I mean, can you see us climbing into that man's van?"

"We could dial like he said, and see what happens."

"Dial what? He never did give us a number, and it's not on the coupon either."

"Maybe he's in the phone book," Marcus said. "Let's go back and try."

Dawn shook her head. "Not with Uncle Doo around. He always says 'don't' no matter what we do."

She hesitated, bent down to pick up a shell. "You wouldn't happen to know how long he's at the library?"

"Until lunch. He told the piano lady he had to leave on time to give us lunch."

As they ran home, flocks of scavenging gulls flapped skyward with shrill, sad cries.

Dawn arrived first. Hurling herself through the front door, she picked up the phone and dialed at random. Marcus followed close behind, flushed with fury.

"I get to dial! It was my coupon!"

Dawn held the receiver tightly with both hands. "Oh, yeah? I bet you haven't even thought who you're going to wish for."

"I've thought of a hundred people. Maybe two hundred."

"Like who?" she demanded. "Name me three."

31

She stood with her ear glued to the receiver until at last she hung up in disgust.

"Nothing! Just one of those dumb recordings that says to verify the number."

"What did I tell you?" Marcus said smugly.

They leafed through the phone book and the yellow pages, but couldn't find any 20th Century Bros Removers. Marcus tried a few numbers unsuccessfully while Dawn, who was losing interest, walked over to the side door that Uncle Doo had told her not to fool with.

"Come look at Uncle Doo's garden!" she cried after she had unlocked the door and wrenched it open.

In addition to the flowers, the bench, and the sundial she had seen the night before, there was a pool the size of a washbasin in which a pink plastic flamingo stood on a single reedlike leg.

Marcus took one look and turned away. "It's tacky."

Dawn was indignant. "What do you mean? I think it's beautiful! And that sundial looks antiquê. We ought to have one in our garden at home. How does it work?"

"It doesn't," said Marcus. "There isn't any sun."

"I know that. But how does it work when there is?"

"By the shadow," Marcus explained. "I learned last year, in science. Here, I'll show you."

He stepped into the garden, carefully avoiding Uncle Doo's dahlias. "See this spiky thing? Well, when the sun's out, it makes a shadow on the dial. If it's here, say"—he pointed to the Roman numeral XII—"that means it's noon."

"Or maybe midnight," said Dawn.

Marcus gave her a scornful look. "Since when is the sun out at midnight? Anyway, Uncle Doo has the thing all wrong. It ought to be pointing in the other direction."

The instant Marcus had turned the dial on its pedestal,

32

the children heard the heaving rumble of a truck pulling into the parking lot. They recognized it immediately. They also recognized the bald-headed driver climbing down from the cab.

"Well?" said Mr. Bros.

Dawn's legs felt strangely shaky. "Well what?"

"You dialed. Has the young gentleman made up his mind? If so, make it snappy. It's not as if he were one of my regular clients. Besides, I'm late."

His engine was still running. Would he drive away? Dawn looked pleadingly at Marcus, but she doubted he knew someone else's Heart's Desire. "Don't go!" she begged. "Marcus has thought of a hundred people. Maybe two hundred."

Marcus moved so close to his sister that the touch of his skin made the hair bristle on her arm. "Only one," he said. "Uncle Doo."

"Your great-uncle?" Mr. Bros raised an eyebrow. "Do you know his Heart's Desire?"

Dawn remembered her promise to bring the old Uncle Doo back to life, but she couldn't think how. She was startled when Marcus said, "He wants to play the flute."

Mr. Bros frowned in momentary concentration. "It's a long way back to that one. A long, long way. That's 1903— almost as far back as I go. But I'll take the job. No choice, now you've got the coupon."

Dawn panicked. "Wait a minute! We're not driving anywhere with you. No way!"

Mr. Bros looked over his shoulder as he climbed into the cab. "No one," he said, "and that means *no one,* rides in my van."

Dawn felt herself shrinking with disappointment as the van pulled away. Then the shrinking feeling turned to

33

wonder. Where the van had been, instead of the south side of the parking lot, was the inside of somebody's living room. It was a stuffy room, full of heavy furniture, with red velvet curtains at every window. Rolled-up rugs were pushed against the walls. Trunks and packing boxes crowded the floor. Books were piled here and there, and the chairs were heaped with winter coats. The room was quiet except for the ticking of a clock on the mantelpiece. While Dawn stood holding her breath, the clock struck nine.

"Morning or night?" Marcus whispered.

Dawn felt like shaking him. "Who cares?" she hissed. "Look what you did, you big baboon! What's this business about Uncle Doo playing the flute?"

Marcus gave her an injured look. "He told you last night at the concert. It was all I could think of."

Dawn could have kicked herself for not thinking of it first. "Do you think we're in a time warp?" she asked, changing the subject.

"It looks like an ordinary house to me," Marcus said, "except people are moving in."

"Well, wherever we are, it's wasting the coupon. If Uncle Doo wants to play the flute, I'll give him mine when Mom and Dad get back from Key West."

"It was my coupon," Marcus reminded her. "I got to choose the Heart's Desire, and I chose this."

Dawn started to argue but stopped when she heard voices outside the room.

"Quick, behind the curtain!"

The voices belonged to a man and a woman, and it soon became clear that the things in the crowded parlor were being moved out, not in.

"This lot seems pretty well in order," the man's voice said. "The books will have to be crated, of course. Have you put aside any pictures that you want to keep?"

"I don't intend to keep a single one of them," the woman's voice answered with a touch of a whine. "They're ridiculously out of date. I'll just save dear Mama's wedding portrait, in the silver frame."

Dawn squinted through a gap in the curtains. The couple were the age of her own parents, but their clothes belonged to another era. The man wore a stiff, white collar. His hair was slicked down sideways across his scalp, and he had a little, pointy mustache. The woman's floor-length dress was very billowy at the bosom, very pinched in at the waist, and dripped with so much lace that Dawn thought she looked like a fancy pincushion.

"Let me see!" Marcus whispered. Dawn let him look through the gap, but she cupped her hand over his mouth and kept it there, in spite of his indignant wriggling.

"The rolltop desk goes to your brother, of course," the man said. "You didn't want it, did you?"

"No, Arthur is welcome to it," the woman replied. "I must have the flower stands, though. I know dear Mama intended me to have them after she passed away. And the sewing table, naturally, and the Chippendale chairs, and the piano."

The man laughed. "I'm not sure Arthur would agree on your dear Mama's intentions. At the funeral, he made it quite clear that she intended him to cart off everything of value in the house."

"Two can play at that game. What could Arthur possibly want with the piano?"

"My poor Delia! What could *you* possibly want with it? We have one already, and we'd never find room in our house for another."

Delia sighed. "In that case I'll take poor Papa's flute."

Her husband's voice sharpened with irritation. "What the devil for? Are you planning to raise Bessie and Char-

35

lotte to be a couple of blue-stocking musicians? Judging by their screams, I assure you they're completely tone-deaf."

Delia sniffed. "I can see you don't care for your daughters, but what if we have a son? I know you, John—you'd want nothing but the best for him."

"The best would never be a flute," said John. "No son of mine is going to grow up a sissy."

He bent down and wrote something on one of the packing boxes.

"Really, dear! Are you insinuating that poor Papa was a sissy?"

The children could hear John and Delia quarreling long after they had left the room.

Marcus pushed through the curtains. "It's a cinch! All we have to do is take that flute and make tracks for home."

He rummaged feverishly in the packing box that the man had marked. "Here it is! And a whole heap of sheet music. Get a load of the funny lady on the cover of this one—gross! She ought to go on a diet. And look, a Polaroid camera!"

Dawn knelt on the floor. "Polaroid? Oh, you dope! That's no camera. Whoever saw a camera made of wood?"

"It's a camera, all right," Marcus said. "Here are all the pictures someone took. It's like at home—two prints for the price of one, except that these are more like postcards."

"I guess nobody had invented color yet, back then." Dawn studied a picture of camels in front of a pyramid, in duplicate.

Marcus tucked the flute under his arm, stood up, looked around. "Let's go. Which door?"

They tried the door the couple had gone through, but

36

found themselves in a dark hallway. All the other doors led into cupboards.

"See what you did?" Dawn's voice trembled. "We're stuck in a time warp. Maybe we're here forever!"

Marcus was pale but stubborn. "Round trip he said, as long as it was someone else's Heart's Desire. We just have to find the way out."

"Well, I'm not going into that hall—it's too spooky. Besides, we'll get caught."

Marcus went back to the window. "Dawnie, there's the van!" he called excitedly.

Together, they shoved open the window and leaned out. The van was parked so close that it blocked the view. Mr. Bros leaned against the side, tapping his foot with impatience.

"Got it?" he asked.

"Got it," said Dawn.

Mr. Bros shifted his weight and yawned. "Well then, put it back."

Marcus nearly dropped the flute in his surprise. "Put it back? What for?"

"Can't bring things through. You ought to know that. We're not movers—we're removers."

"But what's the point, then?" Dawn said. "What's the point of finding Uncle Doo's Heart's Desire if we can't bring it home to him?"

Mr. Bros heaved a mighty sigh. "I can see this is going to be one of my less pleasant jobs. Serves me right for leaving my coupons around for any fool to take."

"One Heart's Desire, round trip," Dawn reminded him. "You promised."

"Used to having your own way, aren't you!" said Mr. Bros. "No effort—tough parts chewed up for easy digestion, bones removed."

37

Dawn felt swollen with indignation. What did he know about her? What right had he to assume her life was easy? He was just like her parents. Did they realize that she spent most of her time worrying? Of course not! They thought she was lazy, and Marcus was cute and bright, and that was the end of it.

"Any suggestions?" she asked.

"Go back," said Mr. Bros. "Go back and think it out. But hurry! I'm due in Schenectady at noon—1927."

The children retreated silently into the parlor and sat down.

"He's crazy," Marcus said after a while.

Dawn shrugged. "He may be crazy, but he's the only person who can get us home."

"Sure, but without the flute."

Dawn walked over to the packing box. She was tucking the flute back into place when she noticed the writing on another box and gave an excited squeak. "Doolittle! Look at that box, Marcus. It says 'Doolittle, Concord Street, Waltham.' "

"So what?" Marcus asked dully.

"So plenty! Look—half these boxes say 'Doolittle, Waltham,' and the others, like this box with the flute, are for that lady's brother Arthur. I bet 'Doolittle' means Uncle Doo's family, so maybe we're just supposed to make sure the flute goes back to them instead of to Arthur."

Marcus's face sweetened with sudden interest. Joining his sister, he studied the labels on the packing boxes. "You're right. Let's switch!"

They chose a box labeled 'Doolittle, Waltham' that was the same size as the one with the flute. It contained a leather-bound set of the complete works of William Shakespeare.

"They'll never miss it, there are so many books already," Dawn said. "Even if they do, they can get it again in paperback for a whole lot cheaper."

"Besides," said Marcus, "Uncle Doo has the exact same set in the bookcase next to the T.V., I noticed."

Working fast, they emptied each box into the other and sealed them both up tight. When they had finished, they hurried to the window. Dawn scrambled over the sill, dropped to the ground, and helped Marcus to follow after.

"Is that okay?" she asked breathlessly. "The way we did it this time, I mean?"

Her only answer was a surly grunt. Mr. Bros drove away, revealing the parking lot of Sunset Grove Arcade. Dawn turned to look behind her, but instead of the window she had just climbed out, she saw Uncle Doo's garden with its flowers, its pool, its bench, and what appeared to be a perfectly ordinary sundial.

Dawn expected to find Uncle Doo playing the flute when they went inside, but he was still at the library. He didn't come home until noon, and she thought he looked depressed and tired.

"Was it a busy morning?" she asked politely.

"About usual," said Uncle Doo. "Two vacationers to see the shell collection, and someone who needed directions to the post office."

"It sounds boring," Dawn said. "Why do you do it?"

"Keeps me busy," said Uncle Doo. "Ready for lunch?"

Dawn followed him to the kitchen, trying to gather courage to ask him about the flute. "Music would keep you busy too," she said at last. "You could join a chamber group."

Uncle Doo was reaching into the freezer, but he pulled his arm out again and shut the freezer door. "I beg your pardon?"

"A chamber group," Dawn repeated bravely. "You know. You could play your flute."

Uncle Doo's face hardened. "What flute? If this is a game, go play it with your brother. I have no time for make-believe."

Four

"I don't know how I got into this," Dawn grumbled. "It's Uncle Doo's Heart's Desire, not ours, and after all that trouble he didn't even get it."

"Something must have worked, though," Marcus pointed out, "because those books were gone. It's funny how he never noticed!"

"I'm not sure," said Dawn. "If they never went to his family after all, back in 1903, he never had them here in Sunset Beach, either. But in that case, where's the flute?"

Dawn was washing the breakfast dishes, to please Uncle Doo. Earlier she had watered all the houseplants. Unfortunately, none of them were real. The plastic imitations were no worse for a soaking, but the ones made of silk were ruined. Instead of pleasing Uncle Doo, she had made things worse.

"I keep thinking it didn't really happen," Marcus said, dreamily wiping a dry plate with a wet dish towel. "I mean, all that way back—1903, Mr. Bros said, didn't he?—and we do something that changes yesterday."

"It happened all right. Only we changed it the wrong way." Letting a glass slip back into the sink, Dawn spun around with a sparkle in her eyes. "Maybe it wasn't wrong. Maybe we just didn't change it enough, and we ought to go again!"

"Would he let us?" Marcus peered into the soapy water. "I think you broke that glass."

The rain had continued through Saturday night, but this morning was clear and sunny. Outside, colors were so sharp that the flat, green blades of palm trees sliced into the flat, blue sky. Dawn reached up and tugged at the curtain over the sink, leaving soapy fingerprints on the cloth. A few feet away from her, out in Uncle Doo's miniature garden, an egret was stalking a lizard. As the curtain moved, the white bird cocked his head at the window, holding his elegant, curved neck absolutely still.

Dawn grabbed Marcus's elbow, warning him to be quiet. The egret took two strides, his long-stemmed legs bending backward at the knee. Then his head shot forward. In his beak was a squirming panic of legs and lashing tail.

Dawn shuddered, horrified but unable to keep from looking at the battle. Twice the lizard got away and twice he was caught again before he stopped struggling and the egret swallowed him whole.

Marcus let out his breath. "That was one mean bird!"

"He can't help it," Dawn reminded him. "It's nature. Animals eating other animals and all that."

"Yes, but when does the lizard get to eat the heron?" Marcus asked.

"He doesn't. He only gets to pick on littler things. Anyway, that was an egret, not a heron."

"That was no egret!"

"Yes it was. What do *you* know about it?"

"More than you do, anyway."

Uncle Doo loomed up behind them and drew the curtain back across the window. "Don't fool with the drapes."

Dawn sighed. "Sorry, Uncle Doo."

"That bird out there is a heron, isn't he?" Marcus demanded.

"Egret." Uncle Doo fished into the soapy dishwater, brought out three shards of broken glass, and dropped them gingerly into the trash.

"Sorry, Uncle Doo," Dawn repeated dully, waiting for the same devastating comment she had received after watering the plants.

The comment never came. Instead there was a glimmer of a smile on Uncle Doo's face as he said, "Broke a few glasses myself, when I was your age. Comes from looking out the window when you should be looking in the sink. Pay attention, next time."

Dawn changed the subject. "When were you my age?"

Uncle Doo's eyebrows shot up. "I beg your pardon?"

Dawn blushed. "I didn't mean to be rude and ask how old you are or anything. I just wondered what year you were born."

"Nineteen-oh-five," said Uncle Doo.

Marcus groaned. "Not until 1905? That's no good!"

Uncle Doo kept a straight face, but his eyes looked amused. "Sorry to disoblige you. What's this all about?"

"Nothing," Dawn said quickly. "It's a sort of game we were playing, and we thought maybe you could help us.

43

Like for instance, does 'Bessie and Charlotte' mean anything to you?"

"About as much as you mean to Marcus. They were my sisters."

Dawn and Marcus stared at each other in embarrassment. They both wanted to know more, but what if Uncle Doo found out about Mr. Bros and the sundial?

"I bet you're wondering how we knew," Marcus said, blurting out the very question he was afraid Uncle Doo would ask.

Uncle Doo shrugged. "I assume you've been looking at the family Bible. Which reminds me: When you're through washing up, better get ready for church."

"Church?" Marcus wailed. "But it's vacation!"

Uncle Doo's mouth twitched as he left the room. "Shoes and socks," he said sternly, "and a dress for Dawn. I'm going for a stroll, to buy the paper."

"He's impossible!" Dawn said, after she heard the front door shut. "One minute he's mean—how was I supposed to know those flowers were silk? They looked real!—and then when I break a glass he doesn't even care. He's like nobody I ever met before."

"He's like you," said Marcus.

"Like me? You're crazy!"

Marcus shook his head. "First you're nice to me, then you're mean to me, and it never has anything to do with what I do myself."

"Want to bet?"

"No," said Marcus. "Whenever we bet, you fix it so you win. You probably cheat."

Fuming inside, Dawn turned her back and let the water out of the sink. "Hurry! If we move fast, we'll have time before he gets back."

44

"Time for what?" Marcus asked, dropping the dishcloth on the floor.

"To go back to 1905, of course. What was the use of 1903 if Uncle Doo wasn't even born yet? That Mr. Bros didn't know what he was doing. Quick, get me the Bible."

Uncle Doo's family Bible was old and leather bound, like the volumes of Shakespeare that, until the day before, had stood beside it on the shelf. Dawn flipped open the cover and pointed to a list of names and dates, inscribed in a careful, old-fashioned script.

"See? 'Delia Kerrigan m. John Doolittle, 1893.' The 'm.' is for married. They must be the ones we saw with the packing boxes. And look, there's a girl named Elizabeth born in 1895, and then Charlotte in 1898. That's got to be the girls they were talking about. And remember how the lady kept saying they might have a son? Well, here he is: 'Elroy—November 3, 1905.' "

"Elroy?" Marcus giggled. "No wonder he wants to be called Uncle Doo. Can you imagine calling him Uncle Elroy?"

He ran down the list of names with his index finger. "There's one more after Elroy, born in 1907. Her name is just plain Nell."

"Who cares about his sisters?" Dawn closed the Bible and shoved it back into place on the shelf. "Let's get moving. If we don't go right this minute, it'll be time for church."

Mr. Bros was visibly annoyed. "What's the problem now?"

In spite of her hurry, Dawn stopped to stare. "You changed your clothes!"

Yesterday and at the concert he had been dressed informally. Today the truck driver wore a three-piece suit, a bow tie, and a bowler hat.

Mr. Bros flicked a speck of dust off his lapel. "Naturally. I'm going to church, like yourselves."

Dawn was confused. "Do you live in Sunset Grove?"

"Heaven forbid!" Mr. Bros said with horror in his voice. "I was referring to the Cathedral of Saint John the Divine in New York City. I'm due there this very instant. Would you kindly state your business?"

"We need to go to 1905, and could you please hurry?"

Mr. Bros shook his head. "One coupon, one round trip. Which is more than you deserved."

"But I never got the Heart's Desire," Marcus argued, "and it's all your fault. Uncle Doo wasn't even born in 1903. I bet you knew it the whole time!"

"And you know better? All right, have it your own way. Do you have a specific day in mind?"

"How about the day he was born?"

Mr. Bros looked shocked. "I hardly think you would like to be in at the birth. Will a christening do?"

"Sure," Marcus said impatiently. "Whatever. Just hurry."

Mr. Bros dusted the driver's seat before climbing back into the cab. "Very well. You'll live to regret it, but there's no time for discussion. I'm late for church."

Dawn and Marcus were inside again, but not in someone's home. Six people were grouped on a raised platform. They didn't speak, didn't move, didn't even blink. At first Dawn thought they were dress dummies.

Standing behind the others was the man named John. He had shaved his mustache, and wore a stand-up collar with the points bent down. His hand was firmly clasped on his wife's shoulder, but he gazed into space with a glassy-eyed expression.

Delia's hair was brushed up in a puffy cloud, topped by a twisted knot. She sat on a green plush sofa, with a baby on her lap. The baby was tiny, and it was wearing a white dress with a skirt so long that Dawn thought you would have to cut off at least a yard of it before you could see the baby's feet.

Also in white dresses, with gigantic pink bows in their hair, were two girls. Their legs, in wrinkled white stockings, were crossed at the ankles, and their hands crossed on their laps. They looked bored.

"Smile please!" said a muffled voice. "Now, one—two—three!"

There was a flash and a burning smell. A photographer emerged from under a small tent of black cloth. "Could we try to look a touch more cheerful?" he asked, wiping his face with a crumpled handkerchief. "This is a christening, remember, not a funeral!"

John and Delia readjusted their mouths into smiles, but the little girls ignored him. "Look, Charlotte!" said the older one. She pointed straight at Dawn and Marcus.

Charlotte bounced on the sofa and squealed. "Please, sir, when you're done with us, could we watch you do their portrait? What funny costumes! What are they meant to be?"

The photographer stared, then moved toward Dawn and Marcus with a menacing look on his face.

"I think we made another mistake," Dawn said, backing away.

"What are we waiting for, then?" asked Marcus.

They turned and fled, opening the first door they saw. It was the darkroom. Fumbling their way through, they

47

left a wreckage of spilled chemicals and broken glass behind them. The photographer followed, shouting with rage. Dawn could feel his hot breath on her neck as she reached out and miraculously touched another door handle.

"My, my!" said Mr. Bros. "That was quick. Found what you wanted? Or did you decide to go to church after all?"

Dawn glared.

"If so, make it snappy," Mr. Bros said, hoisting himself into the van. "You'll need to change. You've spilled something nasty on your skirt."

The skirt was ruined. Dawn rinsed and scrubbed it, but the cloth turned yellow and seemed to rot away. The chemical must have been very strong, she decided, because even after she had washed her hands with soap, her skin burned and tingled all the way to church.

The pews had been rearranged since Friday's concert, and were now respectably lined up to face the altar. The piano had been removed. Miss Purvis, soberly dressed, was seated at the organ, playing hymns. Dawn and Marcus sat with Uncle Doo. A densely sweet smell of jasmine oozed through an open window, making Dawn feel slightly sick. Uncle Doo smelled of Old Spice shaving lotion, which made her even sicker.

Kelly and Lisa sat in the pew behind them. Dawn was careful not to turn around. She leaned back and half closed her eyes. Would she ever grow as plump as Miss Purvis? How would it happen: gradually over the years so she didn't notice until one morning she looked in the mirror and had to face the facts? Marcus had said she was the wrong shape for a ballerina. But ballerinas worked so hard, they didn't have time to get fat. Too hard, maybe. It looked

48

easy onstage, but all that practicing! You had to practice the flute, too, but at least you could sit down while you did it. Uncle Doo wished he played the flute. What was stopping him? Grown-ups could do whatever they liked, and Uncle Doo had been a grown-up for years. How many years . . . ?

Within ten minutes, Dawn was asleep.

She was relieved when the service was over. Circling around Uncle Doo, who had stayed to chat with friends, she and Marcus slipped off to the foyer to study the notices on the parish bulletin board.

" 'Tuesday Night Bingo,' " Marcus read. " 'Prizes.' Should we go?"

"With senior cits? Big deal!"

" 'Free counseling on tax returns,' " Marcus read. " 'Discussion Group: Is There Life After Death?' 'Aerobics for the Elderly.' Do you suppose Uncle Doo does aerobics?"

"I can just see him!" Dawn clutched her stomach and doubled up in a fit of giggles.

Marcus gave a whoop of laughter. "I bet they all do it! Uncle Doo, and the minister, and that fat Miss Purvis—"

A voice behind them interrupted gently. "Your great-uncle doesn't go in for aerobics, but I myself enjoy the class enormously."

The children jumped around and found themselves face to face with Miss Purvis.

"One thing you should always remember," she continued in the same gentle voice. "In every fat old lady, there's a skinny little girl trying to get out."

Marcus took a very large breath and spoke in a very small voice. "I'm sorry."

"Never mind," Miss Purvis said. "I have to admit, it's funny."

49

She reached over the children's heads and carefully removed the notice of next Friday's concert from the board. In its place she thumbtacked another. The first, Dawn remembered, had announced the recital of a local soprano, to be accompanied by Miss Purvis herself. The new notice simply read, "Community Sing: Christmas Carols."

"What happened?" Dawn asked.

"Mrs. Abrams broke her hip. She's in the hospital, poor thing. Not a very cheerful place to spend the holidays! But everybody loves carols, especially if they can join in. I hope you'll come and bring your great-uncle."

"I don't think Uncle Doo can sing," Marcus said. "He just pretended with the hymns today. Anyway, he'd rather play the flute."

Miss Purvis smiled. "I know that, dear. I've known him all my life, and he's been wishing he played the flute ever since I can remember."

"All your life? You mean, when you were a skinny little girl, even?"

Miss Purvis nodded.

"But he didn't live here then," said Dawn. "He lived in Massachusetts."

Miss Purvis folded the old concert notice and tucked it into her purse. "True, and so did I. That's where you two are from, isn't it? Sometimes I miss it—especially at this time of year."

Dawn pictured for a moment what the day would be like at home. If she had been at church, she would walk home along snowy sidewalks, rather than drive down Sunset Parkway in an air-conditioned car. On the other hand she might be sledding, or just reading a book in front of the fire.

"I miss it too," she said, trying to swallow the lump in her throat.

Miss Purvis looked shrewdly at her face. "However, I keep reminding myself that New England can't be much like Bethlehem. If anything, we're closer to it here in Sunset Grove. Now, if I were you two, I wouldn't wait for your great-uncle's car. You've got young legs—why not walk home along the beach? I'll tell Elroy."

She turned to go, but Marcus caught her sleeve. "Wait! Did Uncle Doo ever take flute lessons?"

Miss Purvis hugged her pocketbook to her pillowy bosom and smiled. "No, dear, but his sister did."

"His sister Bessie?"

"His sister Nell."

Dawn nudged Marcus sharply in the back, but he didn't take her hint.

"How come?" he demanded. "If he wanted to so badly, why didn't he learn?"

Miss Purvis sighed and shut her eyes, as if she were looking inward to the past. "When you're young, life seems so long—you think whatever you want is bound to happen eventually. Then suddenly you're old, and it hasn't happened after all, and it's too late."

Dawn wriggled impatiently. "When I want to do something, I do it."

"Do you really?" Miss Purvis opened her eyes again. "What are you doing right now?"

"Talking to you, of course."

"Of course," Miss Purvis agreed. "But with your life, I mean. Do you know what you want to do, and are you doing it?"

Dawn shrugged. "It's different for me. I'm still young."

"Exactly what I was saying, if you think about it," Miss Purvis said. "Elroy was young once too, but he had a harder time than some of us. His father had no use for what he called 'the womanly arts,' as I remember."

51

"Preach, preach, preach!" Dawn grumbled as she trudged along the beach, swinging her shoes by the laces. "Why did you ask all those questions? You could have given us away."

"I wanted to know," said Marcus. "I still don't understand."

"I don't either," Dawn admitted. "I was thinking the same thing in church. It seems like an awful waste of a Heart's Desire. If he wanted it so badly, why couldn't he have done it himself?"

"Remember what the piano lady told us about that man John?" Marcus said. "No son of his was going to grow up a sissy. What's so sissy about playing a flute?"

"You're right. Most of the really famous flute players are men anyway. Look at James Galway, and those Frenchmen."

"I bet John Doolittle would say Frenchmen are sissies too," said Marcus.

"What a jerk!" Dawn kicked viciously at an abandoned sand castle, scattering turrets and crenelated walls.

The beach was still empty, although it was warmer than the day before. Sea gulls and white-winged terns wheeled over their heads. Trim little sandpipers skittered along the water's edge, chasing the waves in and out stiff-leggedly, as if they had been told to walk, not run.

"Too bad Delia married him," Dawn said. "He sounds like a terrible male chauvinist to me. And now Uncle Doo—I mean, he's an old man, and he never got his Heart's Desire, all because his father thought music was a womanly art."

"Womanly art, womanly fart!" Marcus laughed so hard he got the hiccups.

Dawn gave him a quelling look. "What I mean is, it's too bad Delia didn't marry someone else."

"Eighteen ninety-three," said Marcus.

Dawn stopped and stared at him. "What?"

"Eighteen ninety-three," Marcus repeated. " 'Delia Kerrigan m. John Doolittle, 1893.' That's the year she didn't marry somebody else."

Dawn's face widened into a wicked grin. "We changed the books. First Uncle Doo has twenty volumes, leather bound. Next thing you know, bingo! They're back in 1903. Let's get rid of John Doolittle."

Marcus gasped. "You wouldn't!"

"Well, don't look at me as if I were a criminal," said Dawn. "I'm not planning to murder the guy."

Sunset Grove Arcade loomed up on the horizon. A cloud covered the sun, and Dawn felt chilly again as the wind whipped her dress around her thighs. She quickened her pace, and Marcus hurried after her. Behind them church bells were laboriously tolling out "God Rest Ye Merry, Gentlemen." The tolling was thick with scratches. Even from a distance Dawn could tell they weren't real bells but only a broadcast recording.

Mr. Bros wore a gray silk dressing gown, over blue silk pajamas. His face was stern.

" 'God blessed the seventh day and sanctified it,' " he quoted. "Haven't you children any respect for the sabbath? Put that sundial back properly, please. It's about to topple off."

Dawn did as she was told. "We're sorry to disturb you," she began.

She was distracted by the silk pajamas. How could anyone drive a truck dressed like that?

53

"Then why do it?" Mr. Bros snapped.

Dawn took a deep breath and started over. "It's just that I had an idea. Or I guess maybe it's partly Marcus's idea. At least, he put it in my head."

Mr. Bros looked crosser than ever. "Out with it. Quit shilly-shallying."

"We'd like 1893, please," said Dawn.

"You'd like 1893 what?"

"We need to go back there," Marcus explained. "Dawn thinks she can unmarry Delia Kerrigan."

"Not unmarry, stupid," said Dawn. "Find her someone else, is all, who doesn't think flutes are sissy."

"Well, that's unmarrying her from someone who does, isn't it?"

"No, smarty-pants, because this way she never would have married him in the first place."

"But she did—"

"No she didn't—"

"Hold it!" said Mr. Bros. "No go."

The children looked at him in disbelief.

"Why not?"

"Can't you read? 'EST 1901,' it says, plain and clear."

" 'Est' means established," Marcus said.

"So it does. As well as 'estimated,' and 'estuary,' and 'Eastern Standard Time,' to say nothing of 'Erhard Seminar Training.' That's beside the point."

Marcus sighed. So far his mother had been wrong about everything written on the truck: "Removers," and "Bros," and "Dial," and now "Est."

"Then what *does* it stand for?"

"Earliest Search Terminus," said Mr. Bros. "Luckily for you."

"Why luckily for me?" Marcus asked.

"Because if you unmarried Delia Kerrigan, as you so naïvely put it, you'd upset the whole apple cart, that's why. She wouldn't have the same children. Might not have children at all, have you thought of that?"

Carefully gathering up the folds of his dressing gown, Mr. Bros climbed into the cab and drove away.

Five

"You blew it!" Marcus said with a certain satisfaction.

"Not necessarily," said Dawn.

She held her nose and jackknifed down to the bottom of the pool, deliberately kicking her brother in the stomach while she was at it. Marcus shoved her head under just as she was coming up for air. By the time Dawn surfaced, she had swallowed a lot of water, and was more frightened than she liked to admit.

"I'll get you for that!" she spluttered.

Marcus splashed out of the pool and sat down next to a group of fully dressed adults. Revenge was impossible without soaking five senior citizens to the bone. Dawn

56

gave up and floated on her back, staring dreamily into the sky.

Swimming was easy. Swimming took no effort. And you needed a little flesh on you to keep warm—you didn't have to be skinny like a ballerina. Racing was another question, of course. You had to keep up your muscles. But water ballet?

Dawn Foster pointed her toe at the sky, forming a star with the other swimmers. They wore silver suits—all but Dawn, whose suit was gold. The others drew back, leaving Dawn alone. She raised her arms, then flipped back, slipping underwater, reappearing in a surge of spray. Sleek as a dolphin, graceful as a mermaid, star of the show—

Again she swallowed water. Spitting, choking, she kicked blindly to the side of the pool and gasped for breath. She was ready to kill Marcus, but Marcus was still sitting with the senior citizens, wrapped in his towel. Only Kelly was in the pool. Kelly had dunked her.

Shivering, Dawn hoisted herself out of the pool, snatched her brother's towel, and drew it around her shoulders. "Did you see what happened?"

Marcus nodded. "I tried to warn you, but you didn't hear."

"I'll get back at her. Not now, but when it's warmer. I don't know how they can call this a heated pool."

"It isn't," Marcus said. "The machinery hasn't been working at all since we got here. They only took the cover off for us, so what do you expect?"

"Service," Dawn said loftily. "Listen. You can't say I blew it when it was your idea to go back to 1893. Besides, what's keeping us from trying again?"

"He said to call another company, that's what."

"Only if we wanted to go farther back than 1901. We have to go forward instead, is all. To when Uncle Doo isn't a baby anymore."

"Forward where?"

"I'm not sure," Dawn said. "We had two ideas, and they were both no good."

"But the time Mr. Bros chose where to go, the flute was there and we did something about it," said Marcus.

"Sure. We got ourselves into trouble."

"At least we rescued the flute," Marcus pointed out. "The problem is, it went to Nell instead of Elroy. Maybe *Mr. Bros* should decide where we go next."

"If he comes back."

He didn't. Not that afternoon, nor the next morning either. Whenever they had a chance, the children slipped out to Uncle Doo's garden and turned the sundial, but there was no sign of the Removers van.

There were only three more days until Christmas. On Monday afternoon Dawn settled down to reread *Sara Crewe*, while Marcus pasted shells on empty boxes in a halfhearted attempt at making presents for his parents and Uncle Doo. The weather had grown worse rather than better, so the only other entertainment was television. His favorite shows didn't begin until late in the afternoon.

"Is it time yet?" he asked.

"Look for yourself. I'm busy."

"Not as busy as I am."

Dawn turned a page. "I'm at an exciting part."

"What's happening?"

"Miss Minchin is being really mean. She's making Sara wear her old clothes, and—"

"Big deal," said Marcus. "Could you please check the T.V.? My fingers are full of paste."

58

Dawn switched on the T.V. to see if *Masters of the Universe* had started. "Not yet. After these commercials."

"You want to try the sundial again?"

"Forget it—he'll never come."

"That coupon was a rip-off," Marcus said.

"It sure was," Dawn agreed. "You ripped it off yourself, remember? That's probably why things aren't working out. Poor Uncle Doo!"

She picked up the paste, then dropped it again as she heard the rumble of a motor, followed by a squealing of brakes. Rushing to the window, she looked out and saw Mr. Bros waving at them from the cab of his van.

"Help!" Dawn scrambled to her feet. "What if Uncle Doo sees him?"

They slipped quietly out the front door and ran around to Uncle Doo's garden.

"Why are you here now?" Dawn demanded.

"You dialed," said Mr. Bros.

"But that was ages ago. This morning, and last night. We gave up trying."

"Never give up," said Mr. Bros. "I was in Wayne, Maine, 1993. It took a while to get back."

"You mean you can go into the future?" Marcus's face lit up.

Mr. Bros shrugged. "That depends whose future. If you mean your own, yes. 1993 happens to be my past. We're twentieth-century removers, don't forget."

Marcus turned excitedly to Dawn. "Then why bother with the past? Let's just go to next year and have Uncle Doo already playing the flute."

"Dummy!" Dawn said. "Where do we get the flute?"

"We could wait until Mom and Dad get here and give him yours. You never practice anyway."

59

Dawn shook her head. "Then what? Do we just hand it to him and say 'Play!'? We have to start in the past. We have to track down the other flute, in that box where we put it, back in 1903."

"When you're ready—" said Mr. Bros.

"We're ready now," Marcus told him firmly, "and I have an idea. We want to go back to the earliest time where we can do some good. Lessons, or music school, or maybe we could get that dumb John Doolittle to change his mind. But you choose, okay? Because you're the one who knows."

Mr. Bros nodded and moved toward the van.

"Wait!" said Dawn. "I don't think we're dressed right. Our clothes had a weird effect on those people last time. We won't be more than a minute, I promise."

The last time Dawn had been bare legged, with her skirt far above her knees.

"*You* didn't look too bad," she told Marcus. "Boys' clothes don't change all that much, I suppose. Except you had that *Star Wars* shirt on, and it was kind of wild."

Unfortunately, they didn't have much choice. They had packed for the tropics: the sort of clothes that would look out of place back home in Massachusetts, to say nothing of the past. In desperation, Dawn pulled two pairs of corduroy slacks from the bottom of the suitcase.

"Why don't we wear these, and plain shirts? At least we won't stick out like a sore thumb, and I've got short hair, so maybe they'll think we're both boys."

When the van moved, they were in a cornfield. It was late fall. The stalks had been cut to a foot above the ground. Here and there, between the furrows, small shards of ice were forming in the damp earth. Curled, brown fists of oak leaves still hung from skeletal branches at the field's

60

edge. Back in the trees, the children could see, was a small, screened-in structure like a porch with no house attached. In the distance was a house with smoke rising from each of its three chimneys.

Dawn shivered and stamped her feet. "Lucky we're not barefoot—this is worse than Sunset Beach! Couldn't you have picked a warmer day?"

"I didn't pick at all," Marcus reminded her crossly. "I asked Mr. Bros to pick, remember?"

"Okay, don't get mad. It was a really good idea, I have to admit. And at least it isn't raining."

The sky was almost lavender, rippled with high-flying clouds, and the sun shone through the trees—a late-afternoon sun, whose low, slanting rays turned the stubby cornstalks into gold. Crows circled overhead, jeering at one another. And straining against the sky beyond the crows, a scarlet diamond flirted with the wind, darting this way and that, wheeling and diving.

"Someone is flying a kite," Marcus said. He turned and saw two little girls a hundred yards away.

Dawn caught her breath, then let it out in a relieved sigh. "They're dressed like anybody else."

As the girls ran toward them, winding in the kite string, Dawn changed her mind. They weren't as different as the people in the photographer's studio, but they were different from her friends back home. Their clothes looked heavier, more awkward: knee socks and woolen skirts that turned out to be wide-legged pants when she looked a second time. Their sweaters were too bulky, their long hair was tied back in a way that was out of style at home, and they wore lace-up, leather shoes. She guessed they were Marcus's age, or younger. One was blond. The other had dark hair and pale skin with a sprinkling of freckles.

61

The little girls shouted and waved, then stopped, suddenly bewildered.

"Sorry," said the dark-haired one. "We thought you were Elroy and Mr. Willy."

There was an embarrassed pause.

"Well, we're not," Dawn said. "Who are you? Are you Charlotte and Bessie?"

The two girls burst out laughing. "Elizabeth, my dear!" the dark one chirped, dipping a curtsey while the blond one warbled, "Charlotte, da-a-a-rling!"

"I take it they're not," Marcus whispered.

When the dark girl had stopped laughing, she flopped down on the ground. "You're silly!" she told Dawn. "How could you think we were Charlotte and Bessie? They're old!"

"How old?" asked Dawn.

"Oh, ancient. Grown-up, no-more-fun old. You know, beaux, and balls, and all that. Bessie is twenty. She's engaged to marry, and the wedding is next June."

"But we're never going to marry," the blond girl continued. "Mollyanna and I are going to be best friends forever. We'll run away to sea—next year, perhaps—and stow away and sail to Madagascar, and Paris."

"You can't sail to Paris, Nell," the dark one told her reprovingly.

"Yes you can," said Nell. "Up the river Seine."

"Not in a five-masted schooner."

"I wouldn't try it in a schooner. I'd take the *Mauretania*, first class."

As if on signal, they threw themselves into a series of sloppy cartwheels.

"Did you hear that?" Dawn whispered. "Nell! She was the youngest, in the Bible. She was born in 1907, remember?"

"So was our grandmother," Marcus said, looking dazed. "She's old now. Everybody we meet in this place is grown up in our time, or even dead. I don't think I like it."

For a moment, Dawn's blood ran cold. But the two girls turning cartwheels were so alive that her own time seemed unreal in comparison.

Nell and Mollyanna finally turned right side up and came back to the newcomers. "Who are you?"

"Dawn—" Dawn began.

Marcus interrupted her. "This is Don, and my name is Martin."

Dawn frowned. It bothered her that Marcus had been taking the lead more and more in the past few days, but now wasn't the time to argue. "How old is Elroy?"

"He's ten. His birthday is today. Mollyanna wasn't invited, so we're having our own party in the gazebo, after the nasties go home."

"What nasties? What's a gazebo?" Marcus wished the girls would keep still for a moment so he could get things straight.

"The gazebo is over there," Mollyanna said, pointing at the screened-in structure, "and the nasties are boys. Ten of them. Last year they invited nine, but next year he's allowed eleven. That was Mrs. Doolittle's idea. I think it's silly, don't you?"

"Yes," said Marcus, "because by the time he's eighty-one he'll have to find eighty-one friends."

Mollyanna giggled. "Well, that won't be for years and years. Today he has ten. And Nell, of course, except she was mad at Elroy for not inviting me, so she ran off with his kite. Elroy will be furious!"

"No he won't," Nell said. "He told me I could borrow it. He'll be here himself in a minute, only Mama won't let him come until his guests have left the house."

"But Nell says there's plenty of cake left," said Mollyanna, "and Mr. Willy is bringing lemonade. He's one of Elroy's teachers, and he's nice. Would you like to come?"

"Yes, come!" said Nell.

Scooping up the scarlet kite, she ran toward the gazebo. Mollyanna followed, stumbling over the furrows.

Marcus looked at Dawn. "Should we?"

"Why ask me? You seem to be the boss lately."

"So what? Just because you're older doesn't mean you're the boss all the time."

Dawn opened her mouth to argue, then changed her mind. "We'd better go. If Mr. Bros sent us here, it means there's something we can do. Besides, I liked them. Why did you change our names?"

"Because of Elroy," Marcus explained. "He's Uncle Doo, right? If we tell our real names, when we get back home he might remember us."

Dawn was impressed. "Pretty good! But what if he recognizes us anyway?"

"I bet he doesn't," Marcus said, looking pleased. "Not after all those years. Besides, now you're a boy."

When they reached the gazebo, the second birthday party was in full swing. A cloth had been spread on the floor—a good thing, Dawn thought, considering the number of dead flies lying around—and some chipped china cups and plates set on it. There were the remains of a cake with pink icing, a pitcher of lemonade, and half a dozen oranges. A young man was peeling an orange. The boy in the sailor suit sitting beside him looked so much like a small, plump version of Uncle Doo that Dawn could hardly keep from laughing.

Nell Doolittle looked up from the cake, which she was cutting into messy chunks. "Here they are!" she cried, sending crumbs in all directions. "Don and Martin, meet Elroy and Mr. Willy."

Dawn thrust her hands into her pockets, stuck her chin out, and tried to feel like a boy.

"Are you new in town?" Mr. Willy's voice was muffled; his mouth was full of orange.

Dawn shook her head helplessly. She thought it was odd to say "town" when there was only one house in sight.

"We're visitors," Marcus said.

Mr. Willy swallowed. "Thought so. I don't remember seeing any new boys in the Academy."

Although, judging by the pink icing on his sailor suit, Elroy had already eaten more than his share of cake that afternoon, he reached for another piece.

"Pig!" said Nell. "You'll be sick. Give it to Mollyanna— she didn't get any at the party, and she's all skin and bones."

Mollyanna grinned impishly. "I like being skin and bones. It's better than being plump, like Elroy."

Mr. Willy peeled another orange and passed around the sections. "I'll have him on the team next spring, won't I, Elroy? A little more practice, a little less cake, and you'll slim down in a hurry."

Elroy swallowed his cake in one solemn gulp, as if he weren't enjoying it anymore. Dawn thought it was a pity and wished Mollyanna would leave him alone. Then she remembered that Elroy was her great-uncle, and she nearly choked on her orange section.

"Do you teach sports at Elroy's school?" she asked.

Mr. Willy nodded. "Among other subjects."

"But Elroy hates sports," said Mollyanna. "He's the slowest runner in the Academy, and he can't touch his toes. I've seen him try."

Elroy wiped his fingers on his sailor suit. "You can't

65

have seen me try, because I never *cared* to try. I don't keep my brain in my feet, like some people I could mention."

Dawn remembered how Miss Purvis had said that Uncle Doo didn't go in for aerobics, and she felt sorry for the boy. "What did you get for your birthday?" she asked, to change the subject.

Elroy brightened up and started to talk of books.

"But that was at the party," his sister interrupted. "The best was family presents, this morning. Mama found some old boxes in the attic—things that belonged to *her* mama and papa, that she'd forgotten. Elroy picked first, but the rest of us had presents too. Mine is a flute. It's made of real silver, and I'm learning to play tunes on it."

Marcus looked reproachfully at Elroy. "Nell has it? But you had first choice!"

"There was a stereoscope," Elroy told them happily. "A super one, with piles and piles of views!"

Dawn could have screamed with exasperation. "That wooden thing instead of a flute? What about Bessie and Charlotte? I suppose they divided up the sheet music."

"Nobody wanted the music," Elroy told them. "It was for piano, not flute. They chose from another box: jewelry, and scarves." Then he frowned. "How did you know about the sheet music?"

Dawn and Marcus took large bites of cake and chewed while Elroy waited for an answer. Judging by the suspicious look on Mr. Willy's face, Dawn knew she had better think up a good one.

"Look," she said to Elroy. "The person we're visiting— I'm afraid I can't tell you his name—well, he sent us to talk to you because he knew about the boxes, and he thinks you're making a big mistake. He's heard you—"

Dawn stopped. She had been about to say "singing," but remembered that Uncle Doo had only pretended to sing the hymns in church. "He's heard *about* you, I mean, and he thinks you have hidden talent, so you ought to have picked the flute."

Nell scowled, but Elroy was intrigued. "Why doesn't the fellow come and tell me himself?"

"He wishes to remain anonymous," Dawn told him solemnly. "But it's more important than you imagine. *You must change your mind!*"

Mr. Willy burst out laughing. "Hidden talent? Mysterious strangers? What nonsense! Have you the slightest desire to play the flute, Elroy?"

To the astonishment of everyone but Dawn and Marcus, Elroy nodded seriously.

There was a gleam of interest in Mollyanna's eyes. "Then you should do it, Elroy. Take the flute. Nell doesn't mind."

Nell minded. She stuck out her bottom lip, clenched her fists. "It's not fair!" she cried, her voice rising in anger. "I won't let him—it's not fair!"

Mollyanna grabbed her arm and shook it. "Who cares about the flute? Take the sheet music and we'll both learn to play the piano. Won't that be fun?"

"No," said Nell.

"It would be fun for me," Mollyanna said sadly. "I've always wanted to play the piano."

Nell's face softened, but she repeated, "No."

"I'd trade," Elroy offered. "You can have the stereoscope."

Mr. Willy looked from one to the other in disbelief. "Are you serious? I would have given you piano lessons if you had asked, Mollyanna, and if it comes to that, I can teach flute too."

It seemed too good to be true. "Teach flute?" said Dawn. "But you teach sports!"

"On the side." Mr. Willy's eyes twinkled. "For the benefit of outdoor types like Elroy. But officially, I'm Music Master at the Elmbridge Academy for Boys."

Dawn felt the sudden exhaustion that sometimes comes with relief, but Marcus reminded her of another problem. "It won't work. His father won't let him."

Mr. Willy laughed. "John Doolittle? He won't like it, but don't worry. I'll persuade him. After all, there are advantages to being Sports Master on the side. I'll have a talk with him—how about that, Elroy? But we may have to throw in a little bait. Could you bring yourself to play baseball next spring?"

"No," Elroy said, reaching for the last piece of cake.

He drew his hand back as a woman's voice called shrilly from the main house. "Elroy? El-ro-o-oy!"

Elroy stood up and brushed the crumbs from his sailor suit before shaking hands stickily with Marcus and Dawn. "Where do you live when you're not visiting?"

"Weston, Massachusetts," Dawn said without thinking.

Elroy's face lit up. "Weston? That's not far. Can you come back tomorrow?"

For a moment, Dawn was confused. What was tomorrow—the day after Elroy's tenth birthday party, or a Tuesday in December in Sunset Grove?

Before she could answer, the woman's voice called again and Delia Doolittle, noticeably older and wearing a much narrower skirt, came tripping toward them through the trees.

"El-ro-o-oy!"

"Quick!" said Marcus. "Where's the van?"

Elroy looked startled. "What van?"

"The one we came here on," said Marcus. "I mean, the one we came here from behind."

"Oh, shut up!" Dawn cried. "You'll confuse them. Just follow me."

As she ran toward the cornfield, she felt dizzy with pride and excitement. Elroy had the flute now, and Mr. Willy would give him lessons. When she walked through Uncle Doo's front door, she might hear music!

Six

Rain trickled down their necks and soaked their clothes, but they stood in the parking lot, not daring to go inside. They had been gone much longer this time. Would Uncle Doo be angry? Was he worrying?

"Staying out here won't help," Marcus said. "We could say we just went for a walk."

Dawn shook her head. "In the pouring rain? He'd never believe us. What if he calls up Mom and Dad and says we can't stay here anymore?"

"If we act really sorry, he can't get too mad," Marcus reasoned. "We could say we were at the video arcade. After all, it isn't as if we stayed out after dark."

70

Suddenly he laughed. "Wait a minute. It isn't dark yet! Remember, it was almost time for *Masters of the Universe?* Well, by the time *Masters of the Universe* is over, it's dark outside, so we're not late."

They entered the apartment cautiously and ran to the T.V. set. *Masters of the Universe* was just starting.

"That's impossible!" Marcus said.

"The whole thing is impossible, but this time we did it right. I bet we hear him playing any minute now." Heaving a sigh of relief, Dawn collapsed on the sofa and stared at the screen. Marcus was just settling down beside her when Uncle Doo walked in and switched to another channel.

Marcus let out an earsplitting howl. "Turn it back! Quick, turn it back!"

On the new channel, a symphony orchestra was tuning up and an invisible audience applauded the conductor on the podium.

Uncle Doo glanced briefly over his shoulder. "You might do something about that mess on the floor."

"Mess?" Marcus repeated indignantly. "I'm making Christmas presents!"

"Very nice," said Uncle Doo. "Spread newspapers next time. I hope that white paste is water soluble. You'll find a sponge under the sink."

"I'll do it afterward, I promise, but please can we watch *Masters of the Universe?*"

Uncle Doo didn't reply.

"We got here first!" Marcus said.

The music had started. Uncle Doo turned and glared at the two children. "*Masters of the Universe?* Masters of poppycock! I may never have had the guts to become a musician myself, but at least I can enjoy a concert on my own television set."

71

Marcus was stunned. "You never became a musician? But still, you took flute lessons, didn't you?"

Uncle Doo shook his head impatiently and turned back to the symphony orchestra.

Behind him, Dawn burst into tears.

Uncle Doo had let the children sleep late for the first three days, but the next morning he knocked on their door at eight.

"I'm off to the library!" he shouted. "Could I have a word with you first?"

Marcus stumbled out, bleary-eyed, in his pajamas. Dawn, on the other hand, had been awake for hours wondering why Elroy had never taken lessons after all. They had arranged for him to get the flute and for Mr. Willy to teach him to play it. What had gone wrong? She felt sorrier than ever for Uncle Doo.

"You're looking a little peaky," Uncle Doo said when she came out of the bedroom. "Anything the matter?"

Dawn shrugged.

"Not homesick, are you?"

She no longer knew if she was or not, but in any case that wasn't the problem. She shook her head. "We like it here," she said without much enthusiasm.

"Well, suit yourself," said Uncle Doo. "It's been no trouble having you. I may not show it, but I'm glad of the company. Enjoy it, even!"

Why was he so unpredictable? Dawn couldn't figure him out. Marcus had said she was the same, but it was normal for a girl to snap at her brother one moment and act friendly the next. Why was Uncle Doo that way? Was it because he was old and had never done much with his life? If he had had his Heart's Desire, would he be different? Dawn tried to think herself into Uncle Doo's mind, and failed.

"How can you enjoy our company?" she asked. "We broke a glass, and got glue on the rug, and I watered your silk begonias."

Uncle Doo looked away and cleared his throat. "Place survived the hurricane, didn't it? It'll survive you."

Dawn smiled. She remembered that her mother had suggested helping out. "Did you want us to do something while you're gone? Like vacuum, maybe?"

Marcus looked horrified, and Uncle Doo's eyes flickered with alarm. Dawn had vacuumed once before, but she had snapped the tube into the end that blew out instead of the one that sucked in.

"Thanks anyway," he said, "but you're on vacation, as you keep reminding me. You ought to spend more time on the beach, but it's still raining. A friend of mine offered to drive you around a bit while I'm gone this morning. You might ask Kelly and Lisa to come too."

"No thanks," said Dawn. "We don't need company. We're fine, really. Why don't you tell your friend not to bother?"

"No bother," said Uncle Doo. "It's all planned anyway—too late to change."

"I wonder who his friend is?" said Dawn.

It was Anna Purvis. Unlike Uncle Doo, she drove an ancient Volkswagen. Not only did it not have air conditioning; its windows steamed up if they were shut, but when they were opened the rain blew in sideways. Cars like Uncle Doo's honked as they sped past on Sunset Parkway.

Miss Purvis sat hunched up behind the steering wheel, squinting nearsightedly at road signs. "What does that one

73

say, dear?" she asked, slamming her foot on the brake.

The drivers behind leaned on their horns angrily.

"It says 'No Turn on Red,' " Dawn told her, "but the light's green, Miss Purvis."

"So it is." She accelerated just as the light turned red again, then put her foot on the brake a second time, throwing the children against their seat belts.

"Sorry, dears!"

When Miss Purvis turned onto a quiet side road, Dawn felt like a condemned prisoner who had been reprieved. As if to celebrate, the rain tapered off and there was a sudden gleam of sky between two clouds.

"Just in time!" Miss Purvis said happily. "Not that I mind getting wet, but the animals might have been hiding inside."

"Animals?" Marcus repeated.

"Animals. Tropical Wonders Park, they call it. Only thing I could think of for people your age."

Miss Purvis swung into a parking lot, turned off the ignition, and waited patiently while the motor continued to run for close to a minute. "Engine needs tuning," she told Marcus as she squeezed out from under the steering wheel.

Dawn, following her up a narrow pathway between wet, overhanging bushes, wondered why such a plump old lady chose to drive such a tiny old car.

After that one promising gleam of light, the clouds joined together again and a light drizzle began to fall. In spite of the rain, Tropical Wonders Park was hot and the air thick with stench from the animal cages.

They were the only visitors. Steering clear of puddles, they moved from cage to cage. Returning stare for stare were sodden-winged parrots, lethargic alligators, a pair of

74

skunks, and a puma with a resigned expression on its face.

An employee was filling a bucket near the puma's cage. Dawn walked up to him. "How does that puma get enough exercise in such a tiny little space? Does it ever get to run around free?"

The man straightened up and laughed as if she were more of a show than the Tropical Wonders themselves. "Oh, she gets tired out just pacing back and forth," he said. As if that ought to answer Dawn's question, he went back to work.

Dawn rejoined her brother and Miss Purvis, but her mind was on the puma. How could anyone be cruel enough to keep it prisoner in a space no larger than Uncle Doo's kitchenette? Of course it paced back and forth, but you couldn't call that exercise. She wished she could run back and let it free.

"Don't!" the keeper cried. "That cat's a killer—you're risking death!"

Dawn Foster looked scornfully over her shoulder, walked fearlessly to the cage. "I risk death with every breath I breathe. But in all my career as a famous animal trainer, no beast has ever tried to harm me. They know I'm on their side."

Marcus stood trembling by the keeper, fear and admiration in his eyes.

"Don't be a little fool, Dawn! The world can't afford to lose you."

"Nothing ventured, nothing gained," said Dawn. "Don't worry, I won't let the puma hurt *you*."

"You may not mind getting your own feet wet, but you don't have to splash water all over everyone else," said Marcus.

Dawn blinked several times, stared down at her feet.

"You're standing in a puddle."

"So what? Maybe I like puddles."

Miss Purvis intervened. "Perhaps it's time to leave."

"Good. I don't like that place," Marcus announced as they walked back to the car.

Dawn nudged him, but Miss Purvis didn't seem hurt. "Don't you, dear? I'm not surprised. I don't either."

"Then why did you bring us?" Dawn asked.

"Your great-uncle thought you were looking a little out of sorts. Besides, I wanted to find out more about you, so I said I'd take you in charge for the morning. Now, how about some refreshments?"

She drove to a cafe in Sunset Grove and bought them ice cream. Dawn had expected her to be a tea-and-toast person, but Miss Purvis ordered a piña colada and sipped it with obvious enjoyment.

"Too bad your great-uncle couldn't join us, instead of working at that dreary library," she told the children.

"If it's dreary, why does he do it?" Marcus asked.

"To keep busy, of course. To keep up an interest. It's important, at our age. What a pity he never learned to play the flute!"

"It sure is," Dawn agreed, gloomily mashing her sundae into a pulp. "Too bad he didn't take lessons instead of Nell."

Miss Purvis looked up in surprise. "Nell? She didn't play the flute. Whatever gave you that idea?"

Dawn dropped her spoon. She stooped quickly to retrieve it, and wiped it on a paper napkin before answering. "You told me yourself on Sunday. You said that Nell took flute lessons."

Miss Purvis shook her head emphatically. "Not Nell,

dear. Piano, yes, though only for a month or so. She wasn't musical. It was Elroy who had the flute, but he never learned to play it."

Dawn was silent. She could feel her thoughts resettling slowly, the way the snow resettled when she shook those plastic bubbles containing winter scenes.

"Wouldn't you know!" said Dawn, carefully wrapping the last shell-covered box with Christmas paper from the five-and-ten. "The minute we turn our backs, something goes wrong. I don't see why. After all, now Miss Purvis says Elroy got the flute, not Nell. So how come he never played it?"

Marcus was laboriously printing messages on homemade Christmas cards. Dawn sat on the floor beside him giving unsolicited advice. Across the room, Miss Purvis thumped out Christmas carols on Uncle Doo's white piano. She had stayed on after bringing them home—almost, as Marcus pointed out, as if Uncle Doo had asked her to baby-sit.

"Maybe Mr. Willy just couldn't convince John Doolittle to let him take lessons," Marcus said under his breath. "How many S's at the end of Xmas?"

"One," said Dawn.

"I bet you're wrong. It has to be two, because it means 'mass,' like in church."

"If you're so sure, why ask?"

Marcus shrugged. "I don't care. One S is easier anyway. Where's the purple marker?"

Dawn handed it to him. "What I don't understand is that Mr. Willy promised. He said he'd have a talk with Elroy's father."

"Sure, but only if Elroy played baseball, and Elroy said he wouldn't."

"I don't blame him," said Dawn. "I hate baseball. I hate any kind of sports."

"Then how are you going to be a ballerina?"

"That's different."

"It may be different, but I don't see you practicing."

"What do you know about it?" Dawn picked up a square of pink construction paper and scribbled "Season's Greetings!" with an orange marker pen.

"That's gross!" said Marcus. "I could do better myself."

Dawn ignored him. "I could strangle Elroy! But then I remember he's Uncle Doo, and I feel sorry for him."

Marcus gave a worried glance at Miss Purvis. "Watch out, she'll hear."

"Not while she's making that racket."

"I wish she'd need the ladies' room or something," Marcus whispered. "Because if we want things to work out, we'd better go turn that dial right now and ask Mr. Bros to take us back again."

"I bet she needs it soon. She hasn't been since she drove us to the zoo."

But Miss Purvis played ten more carols before she pushed back the piano stool, walked into the bathroom, and locked the door.

Mr. Bros offered no comment when they asked to go back to the year that Elroy was ten. With a long-suffering look on his face he climbed into the van and drove away, revealing not a cornfield, but the circular driveway at the front of the main house.

It was late winter now, almost spring. The earth had an acid smell that bordered on sweetness, as if one warm day would send it spinning into bloom. The bleached grass of the lawn had an undergrowth of green that throbbed to-

78

ward the morning sunlight. A man and a boy were walking up the drive. Both leaned slightly forward, hands locked behind their backs, feet crunching the gravel in heavy strides. The man's voice was gruff, barely masking irritation. The boy's voice was hurt and proud.

Dawn grabbed her brother's hand and backed into the shelter of a rhododendron bush, stepping on someone's foot in the process.

There was a gasp, followed by a moan. Then a voice said, "Hush! Don't make a sound!"

Turning, Dawn found herself face to face with a woman in a clinging dress, high-heeled shoes, and a little feathered hat pulled down to cover her right eye. She looked totally out of place in a rhododendron bush.

"Are you Bessie?" Marcus asked.

"Don't be ridiculous!" The woman glared, then gave them a sudden smile. "Martin and Don! You came back after all! But what are you doing in this bush?"

The children stared pointedly until she laughed. "Me? I came to help, but I haven't done much good so far."

"Same with us," said Marcus.

"Then hush," the woman said. "They're getting closer."

The sound of crunching gravel grew louder.

"Ten years old!" the man was saying. "Your eleventh year, and still dreaming. It isn't normal and it isn't healthy."

"But sir, you don't understand. . . ."

They were Elroy and his father.

"You're my only son. I've placed all my hopes in you. You must look on it as a challenge, a privilege."

Judging by Elroy's face, he didn't. "You're preaching at me, sir," he muttered.

"A little preaching won't hurt you." John Doolittle patted his son's head. *"Mens sana in corpore sano,"* he quoted.

79

" 'A sound mind in a sound body.' All very well to have your nose in a book, but at the appropriate moment, my boy. You're a good student. I couldn't be prouder, but enough is enough. Success was never built on books, you know. Success is built on action and experience."

"Yes sir," said Elroy.

"You seem to be entirely lacking in ambition," his father continued crossly. "When I was your age, my heart was set on becoming a big-game hunter. Impractical, but normal for a boy. But all you hanker after is music and poetry. You must get it from your mother. Now, the arts are all very well at the appropriate moment—"

They passed the rhododendron bush, climbed the steps to the house, and pulled the front door shut behind them.

"Damn!" said the woman, stamping her foot until one high heel was driven into the earth. "That dreadful man! Now what?"

Before they had time to confer, the door swung open again. Elroy Doolittle burst out and ran back down the drive.

The woman's face lit up, and she clasped her hands in excitement. "That's better! He's going in the right direction, too. Do you really want to help?"

The children nodded.

"Then follow Elroy. He'll slow down once he lets off a little steam. When he does, steer him toward the pond."

"What pond?" asked Dawn.

The woman looked surprised that she should ask. "Don't you know the pond? There's only one. Turn left at the bottom of the drive—you can't miss it. Keep him there until I come. And whatever you do, don't let on you know me."

"How should we know you?" Marcus asked.

The woman grinned at him mockingly. She hurried away, clutching her hat and wobbling precariously as her high heels sank into the lawn.

As the woman had predicted, Elroy soon slowed down. He had been muttering angrily to himself, but now his voice rose until Dawn and Marcus could hear him quite clearly.

"Appropriate moment! Where would we be today if Mozart had composed only at the appropriate moment, sir? Did Bach lack ambition, sir? Did Beethoven build success on action and experience?"

Marcus giggled.

"Poor thing," said Dawn. "I know how he feels. We're out of sight of the house now—let's go say hello."

Elroy was too absorbed to hear them coming up behind. "Still dreaming? What if I am, sir? Dreams make the world turn round. Dreams change night into day in more ways than one. Whereas preaching, sir—"

Hearing Marcus give a snort of laughter, he turned and scowled. Then his face broke into a delighted smile. "You're back! I thought I'd never see you again."

"Don't mind Marcus—I mean Martin," said Dawn. "Were you quoting something just now, or did you make up what you were saying?"

Elroy looked embarrassed. "I don't want to talk about it. You wouldn't understand."

Dawn thought she *would* understand, but changed the subject obligingly. She produced a rush of chatter, keeping Elroy's attention so that he didn't notice when she steered him to the left at the bottom of the drive.

"What's Nell up to these days? And her friend Mollyanna? Is your sister married yet? How's Mr. Willy? Is

81

he still teaching at your school? Did you join the baseball team?"

This last question was badly received. Elroy stopped smiling and eyed her suspiciously. "What's it to you?"

"Nothing. Only I thought you had to do it before your father would let you play the flute."

"He won't," Elroy said. "It's no use trying. No matter what I say, all he does is preach, preach, preach."

He refused to answer questions after that. The three of them continued in silence as they passed a barn and an orchard, before arriving at a large pond.

At first there was no one in sight. Before long, however, the woman appeared on a bicycle, looking absurd in her feathered hat and high heels. For a moment she seemed to be steering toward them. Then she swerved, picked up speed, careened over the bank at the side of the road, and landed with a loud scream in the water.

Marcus gasped. "What does she think she's doing?"

Elroy's jaw dropped. His arms swung limply at his side as he watched her splashing in the pond.

"It did kind of look as if she did it on purpose," Dawn said to Marcus under her breath. "Do you suppose she knows how to swim?"

The woman brushed wet hair from her face and reached for her hat, which was floating away like a boat with a feather for a sail. "Help!" she called robustly. "Can't you see I'm drowning?"

Dawn kicked off her shoes.

"Not you, stupid," the woman snapped. *"Him!"*

She pointed at Elroy.

Suddenly Dawn understood. "What are you waiting for?" she asked, giving Elroy a shove toward the pond.

Elroy hesitated. "You know what?" he said slowly. "I believe that was Charlotte's bicycle."

82

"Oh, for heaven's sake!" said Dawn. "What does it matter whose it is? Aren't you going to save a damsel in distress?"

"Distress? There's no more than two feet of water in that pond," Elroy said. "I'm going to save Charlotte's bicycle."

He took off his shoes and socks. Carefully rolling up the socks, he tucked them into a shoe. He rolled up his trouser legs. By the time he had waded to the spot where the woman was drowning, the water came only to his knees. He fished out the bicycle and hauled it toward shore.

The woman, who had been crouching on the bottom, rose and waded after him. "My hero!" she shrieked.

Looking blankly at her, Elroy wheeled the bicycle away.

The woman emptied the water from her shoes and slipped her feet back in. She shook her hat and put it on, ignoring the water that dribbled from the feather to her nose.

"Too bad," she said. "You boys will have to come back and give an eye-witness account. Mind you make it good!"

"Make what good?" Marcus asked. "Account of what?"

"How can you ask?" she said with a twinkle in her eye. "That young man saved my life!"

Seven

"Do yourself a favor," the woman told Elroy when they turned into John Doolittle's driveway. "Take the cycle back to the shed. They're bound to wonder why I had it."

"I was wondering myself," said Elroy, disappearing through a gap in the shrubbery.

"Mind you come back directly!" she called after him. "Meet us at the front door, or you'll spoil your own show."

She stumbled, and stopped to remove her shoes. "Drat! Strap broke. That always happens with the cheap ones. They're made of cardboard."

"You mean you've done this before?" asked Marcus.

The woman glared at him. "Do you take me for an escaped lunatic?"

84

"Not at all," Dawn said soothingly. "I think it was a good idea. But if you want to look more like a damsel in distress, you should do something about your makeup. The way it is now, they might just laugh."

"Thanks," said the woman. She stopped by the front door, pulled a sodden handkerchief from a sodden pocket, and dabbed at her cheeks. Her face was paler afterward, and a sprinkling of freckles appeared. The handkerchief was streaked with black and pink.

"How's that?" she asked. "Distressful enough? And do you recognize me now?"

Dawn shook her head, but Marcus stared at the freckles and cried, "Mollyanna!"

"At your service. Or at Elroy's service, I should say."

"But you're older now, and Elroy's still the same."

"Of course I'm older, silly! I'm just visiting. The eight-year-old me is in the house with Nell, and I'm afraid Elroy would be upset if he knew there were two of me."

"How could there be—" Dawn began.

"Hush, here he comes!" Mollyanna reached for the brass knocker, gave it three healthy bangs, and waited for the front door to open before crumpling theatrically in a dead faint.

John Doolittle was impressed. He thumped Elroy heartily on the back as Delia, Bessie, and Charlotte fussed around the grown-up Mollyanna, who had been revived with smelling salts and was reclining on a sofa. Nell and the eight-year-old Mollyanna hovered nearby, awed into temporary silence.

"It's true, sir!" Marcus said. "My brother Don and I were walking on the road. We saw the accident. This lady lost control and fell into the pond, and Elroy saved her."

"Where's her bicycle?" asked Nell.

Grown-up Mollyanna smiled weakly at her. "Lost, I fear, in the depths of the pond. But it can stay there, for all I care. I hope I never see another bicycle in my entire life!"

She gave a realistic shudder and glanced appealingly at Mr. Doolittle. "You must be proud of your son. So young, and yet so manly! Not a moment's hesitation—not a thought of the danger to himself!"

Dawn cleared her throat. She thought Mollyanna was overdoing it, but Mollyanna was just getting into full swing. She sat up, put her hand to her forehead, and swayed as if she might faint again.

"The test of true manliness," she told Mr. Doolittle, "is quick and selfless action in a crisis. If I were not totally penniless, I would offer Elroy his Heart's Desire."

Dawn jumped. Heart's Desire? Did Mollyanna have a coupon too? Was that what she had meant when she had said she had come to help?

John Doolittle rested his hand on his son's shoulder. "A courageous act is its own reward, isn't it, Elroy?"

Grown-up Mollyanna shook her head impatiently. "There must be something I can do for him, something he wants—except for money, of course." She glared at eight-year-old Mollyanna, as if commanding her to find the answer.

The little girl was silent for so long that Dawn felt like shaking her. Didn't she remember Mr. Willy and the flute lessons?

"I know something Elroy wants," the little girl said at last in a timid voice. "He wants to learn to play his flute. Couldn't that be his reward?"

John Doolittle's face turned red. Dawn could see his jaw muscles tighten.

For once Elroy used tact. "Would you mind, sir? Success is built on action and experience, you said. This would be

86

both, and I would try to play only at the appropriate moment."

They left the room engrossed in manly conversation. A moment or so later, Delia slipped out also with her older daughters, to boil water for tea.

"Maybe we ought to leave now," Dawn told Marcus. "If we stay any longer, they might start asking questions."

"You're right!" Grown-up Mollyanna leaped off the sofa, grabbed her damaged shoes, and made a dash for the front door.

"Tell them I had an urgent appointment!" she called over her shoulder. "As for you, Mollyanna—if you're not nice to Elroy, I'll come back and slap your freckled face!"

Dawn and Marcus ran after her, reaching the front steps just in time to see her disappear behind a van that was parked in the driveway. But when they followed, she had vanished and they were back in Sunset Grove.

Miss Purvis stayed for lunch. Uncle Doo made frozen fish sticks again, served with the create-a-sauce packet, which he had forgotten to mix with the mayonnaise that creates the sauce. Miss Purvis's nose crinkled at her first bite. She ate half a stick, Dawn noticed, before sliding the rest under a leaf of iceberg lettuce.

"You never could cook worth a damn, Elroy," she said, washing down the taste with a large gulp of iced tea.

Uncle Doo lowered his fork and smiled apologetically. "I never had occasion to learn."

"Nonsense! You've had a lifetime to learn. It's sheer laziness."

"Miss Purvis," Marcus interrupted, "how come you live here too?"

87

"Here in Sunset Grove, dear?" she asked. "Well, why not?"

Marcus spoke indistinctly, his mouth full of fish. "I mean, you knew each other when you were a little girl, but that was in Massachusetts. Did you follow Uncle Doo down here?"

"Marcus!" Dawn turned scarlet with embarrassment.

Miss Purvis laughed. "Your great-uncle isn't the only person here I knew before. But yes, I wouldn't have moved to Sunset Grove if it hadn't been for friends. At our age, friends are everything. Isn't that right, Elroy?"

Uncle Doo nodded silently and wiped his chin.

Miss Purvis sighed. "Christmas Eve tomorrow!"

"So it is."

"Coming to the midnight service?"

"Can't," said Uncle Doo. "These two need their sleep."

Although she felt she had had more than her share of church in the past few days, Dawn promptly objected. "It's only once a year—besides, we can sleep late the next morning."

"If you do, you'll be making history," said Uncle Doo. "First time I ever heard of children sleeping late on Christmas morning. In any case, your parents will be turning up."

"Bring them all!" Miss Purvis said. "Bring yourself, too. There's going to be music—a Bach flute sonata. The flutist can't play worth a damn, but Bach will survive. Too bad *you* don't play anymore."

Marcus had been drinking. He slammed his glass on the table indignantly, splashing milk over his place mat. "But you said—!"

Miss Purvis gave him a mildly reproachful glance. "Said what, dear?"

"Never mind." Dawn kicked her brother under the table. "Mop that up, Marcus, and behave!"

Marcus was outraged. After cleaning up the milk, he flung his napkin on the floor and stamped out of the room. In a moment he was back, however, totally transformed. He picked up the wet napkin, apologized, smiled angelically at his sister, and passed his plate for seconds.

"It's there!" he told Dawn under his breath when she stared at him in disbelief. "There's a flute on the shelf in his bedroom. His door was open, and I looked in."

Hours passed before they were alone again. First there had been the dishes to wash. Then, in spite of a cold mist, they had all gone to walk on Sunset Beach. Uncle Doo brought stale bread in a plastic bag. They stood on the wet sand and fed the gulls.

Dawn was frightened of the birds, which seemed much bigger when they were wheeling overhead, their sharp beaks open, ready to dive and snatch the food. But Miss Purvis took off her shoes and danced about, daring the gulls to feed directly from her hand. She looked happy. She even looked pretty. Dawn stared and wondered why she had never married.

The artificial church bells chimed endlessly through the mist, one carol after another until Miss Purvis clapped her hands to her ears and insisted on going back to play carols herself, to drown out the sound. At six o'clock she was still playing, and Uncle Doo had gone to the kitchenette to see what he could find in the freezer for supper.

Dawn and Marcus sat together on the sofa, watching T.V. with the sound turned down. "She'll never go!" Marcus said glumly.

"It wouldn't make any difference if she did," said Dawn. "Uncle Doo would still be here."

89

"We might get a chance to try tomorrow."

"Christmas Eve? I bet he doesn't go out at all. And Mom and Dad are coming back. Then it'll be too late, and we'll have to go home to Massachusetts."

"He's got the flute now," Marcus said, "and it sounds as if he used to play it. Maybe he could take lessons again, here in Sunset Grove."

Dawn shook her head. "No way! He has to have had a whole lifetime playing. Otherwise it wouldn't count as Heart's Desire."

" 'A whole lifetime to learn,' " Marcus said slowly, thinking of Miss Purvis's words at lunch. "Let's get him cooking lessons while we're at it."

Dawn was too worried to laugh. "Why do you suppose he stopped? And when?"

"Let's ask him."

"Let's not," said Dawn. "We've asked too many questions already. If only they'd go away for a while, Mr. Bros could take us there."

The chance came sooner than they expected. When Uncle Doo announced that he had found some stuffed crab left over from the Fourth of July, Miss Purvis remembered a previous engagement for supper. She picked up her umbrella and hurried out, only to knock on the door again because her Volkswagen wouldn't start.

"It's happened a lot recently," she informed them sweetly. "But I understand that's usual, in winter."

"It may be chilly," Uncle Doo grumbled as he felt in his pocket for his own car keys, "but it's not as cold as all that. I'd say the old heap needed tuning, if I didn't think it belonged in the junkyard."

Two minutes later Marcus turned the dial.

This time Mr. Bros was dressed as Santa Claus. With

90

the curly white wig and a pillow stuffed under his fur-trimmed red jacket, he was almost unrecognizable.

"All right, all right!" he snarled. "Save your breath, I know what you're thinking. It just shows how stupid you are. After all, you're not the only ones with a Heart's Desire at this time of year."

"But we weren't thinking anything!" Dawn protested. "It's just a little unusual, you know."

"What's unusual for you may be usual for me," said Mr. Bros. "Egocentric little brats, aren't you!"

Dawn gave Marcus a warning look.

"You've been really nice about taking us places," she said diplomatically. "We've probably had more than our share, but you see, he hasn't got it yet. I mean, Uncle Doo and his Heart's Desire."

"He's got the flute," Marcus explained, "but he can't play it anymore."

"We think he stopped a long time ago," Dawn continued, "only we don't know when."

"But I bet *you* do," said Marcus, "so could you please send us there?"

Mr. Bros made a face that didn't suit Santa Claus. "Never satisfied! Bottomless pits of greed! Ever hear the tale of the fisherman's wife? She ended up wishing to be lord of the sun and moon, and where did it get her? Back home to her hovel, that's where."

Nevertheless, he moved his van.

Mollyanna was in the gazebo, her chin resting on her knees. She looked like the Mollyanna who had ridden Charlotte's bicycle into the pond. Today, however, she was dressed more sensibly, in slacks and low-heeled shoes. She had been crying, and her cheeks were streaked with

91

paths of gray that came, Dawn suspected, from her eye-lashes.

When she saw the children, she managed only a twitch of a smile. "Back again? You haven't changed."

Dawn was out of breath. It had been much harder to cross the field this time; it was summer and the corn had grown high. She felt sticky with perspiration. Something itchy and possibly alive had fallen inside her shirt.

"You haven't changed either," she panted. "That is, depending on which Mollyanna you are."

"I'm both, of course," Mollyanna said. "It's all a question of where you are in time. Don't you know that?"

"How could we know?" Marcus asked. "Just where in time are we?"

"It's twenty years ago," said Mollyanna. "It's 1922."

"Now, wait a minute!" Dawn protested. She stopped and counted in her head. "That's not twenty years ago, it's sixty-four years ago."

Mollyanna looked surprised. "Really? That means you're travelers too. I should have guessed. When are you from? I was removed from 1942."

Dawn felt dizzy. How could they be all those times at once: 1922, 1942 and 1986? It didn't help when she remembered Mr. Bros saying that 1993 was in *his* past.

"Which of us is real?" she asked.

"I am," said Mollyanna.

Dawn decided not to argue the point. "Why were you crying?"

Mollyanna fumbled in her pocket for a handkerchief and wiped her face. After one look at the handkerchief, she fumbled for a compact and powdered her nose.

"Just as well no one can see me," she said.

"*We* can," said Marcus.

"You don't count," said Mollyanna, snapping the mirror shut.

"Why were you crying?" Dawn repeated.

"Elroy." Mollyanna stood up, turned her back to the children, and stared through the trees at the cornfield. "When I was little, we flew kites in that field."

"I know," said Marcus. "I was there."

"Why *were* you there?" asked Mollyanna. She blew her nose into the handkerchief, leaving the tip of it smudged with gray. "Why are you and Don here now?"

Dawn told her about the coupon and Mr. Bros.

Mollyanna nodded. "I know Mr. Bros. He removes me too. But who is Uncle Doo?"

"He's our great-uncle," Marcus said. "He's also Elroy."

Mollyanna caught her breath, turned pale, and sat down again in a hurry. "Your great-uncle? How old is he?"

"Eighty-one," said Marcus. "This is 1986, you know."

"It's not," said Mollyanna. "Thank God it's not! But Elroy—I mean your Uncle Doo—whom did he marry?"

"Nobody, as far as I know," said Dawn, "and so far he doesn't play the flute."

"Then his whole life came to nothing?" Mollyanna sighed. "Poor Elroy! Why did I ever fall in love with him? Oh, well—*Le coeur a ses raisons que la raison ne connaît point.* That's so true, isn't it?"

"I wouldn't know," said Marcus.

"It's French," said Mollyanna. "I studied French at the Conservatory. It means 'The heart has its reasons that reason doesn't know at all.'"

"Well, I don't know about its reasons either," Dawn said impatiently, "but it sure has its desires, and we're here to make Elroy play that flute."

Mollyanna was astonished. "Flute? You boys came all

93

this way just for the flute? I'm here to make him marry me!"

After a moment of shocked silence, Dawn and Marcus burst out laughing. They laughed so hard that they had to hold their stomachs, so hard that Marcus rolled on the floor.

"There's nothing the least bit funny," Mollyanna said in a pinched voice. "You're being very rude."

Dawn stopped laughing first. "I'm sorry. It was just so unexpected. But if that's what you want, it's okay with us, I guess."

"No it isn't!" Marcus said, suddenly sobering up. "Because that isn't Uncle Doo's Heart's Desire. It's yours. Didn't Mr. Bros tell you if it's your own Heart's Desire, you can't come back? One way, not round trip, he said."

Mollyanna looked confused. "Did Mr. Bros tell you that? I can't think why, unless he was mad at you for some reason. He's usually very obliging, once he has given someone a coupon."

Marcus shuffled his feet. "He didn't exactly give it to me. I sort of took it."

"Sort of? What do you mean? Either he gave it to you or he didn't."

"I stole it," Marcus admitted. "I found it in his van and wrote my name on it."

"No wonder he's mad at you!" said Mollyanna. "An honest person would have given it back."

"Preach, preach, preach!" said Dawn. "Why does everybody preach at us? Where did you get *your* coupon, if it comes to that?"

"I earned it, of course," Mollyanna answered primly. "You have to start by wanting someone else to be happy."

"Even supposing it would make Elroy happy if you married him, it's still *your* Heart's Desire. Marcus was right."

94

"That doesn't matter," said Mollyanna. "Mr. Bros would have explained, if he weren't mad at you. It's all right if it's your own Heart's Desire, as long as it makes someone else happy."

"But if marrying him is all you care about, why did you go to all that trouble arranging for flute lessons last time?"

Mollyanna looked from Dawn to Marcus in bewilderment. "It wasn't the last time for me. I've gone back often since then. You see, I wasn't very nice to Elroy when I was a little girl, and I thought I could change that. So I made me—little me, I mean—the one to suggest flute lessons as a reward."

"Did it make him like you any better?" Dawn asked.

"For a while it did. But I kept forgetting—little me, I mean—and teasing him about being plump. And then I'd have to go back—big me did, that is—and force little me to do something so Elroy would like me again."

Dawn tried to make sense of Mollyanna's story. "It sounds confusing, and it doesn't sound as if it's helping."

"You're right," Mollyanna confessed sadly. "It never did much good. That's why I'm here today."

Dawn groaned. "Just exactly what's wrong today?"

"It's the Elmbridge Academy Senior Summer Ball," said Mollyanna.

"The what?"

Mollyanna repeated it. "And Elroy isn't taking me," she added. "He's taking Lillian Prendergast."

"Big deal!" said Marcus.

Dawn smiled. "You mean you've been making all this fuss just because Uncle Doo took somebody else to a dance sixty-four years ago?"

"Twenty, not sixty-four," Mollyanna corrected her. "And it's worth fussing, because he's going to marry her."

"Marry her?" Dawn shook her head. "How could he?

If this is 1922 he'd be seventeen. No, sixteen, because his birthday isn't until November. That's too young to get married."

"But you don't understand!" Mollyanna cried impatiently. "We're only *visiting* 1922. It's really 1942, and they're engaged."

"Twenty years later?" Dawn asked. "Then they'd both be too old!"

"Don't be childish," said Mollyanna. "You're never too old to fall in love. The point is, I wanted him to fall in love with me, and instead he met Lillian again, when she was a war widow, and he fell in love with *her*."

"Well, I wouldn't worry about it if I were you," said Marcus. "Because actually it's 1986, and Uncle Doo never married anyone."

Mollyanna pounded her fist on her knee. "I tell you, they're engaged, and the wedding is in September." She covered her face with her hands and began to sob.

"Oh, for heaven's sake!" said Dawn. "Stop, or someone will hear you. What do you want us to do, go to that ball and step on Lillian's foot or something?"

"There's nothing you can do." Mollyanna took out her compact again, looked at her face, and moaned.

Dawn thought for a moment. "I can't imagine anyone wanting to marry Elroy, but I have an idea that might help us both. If we take you to that ball, will you promise to find out why he stopped playing the flute?"

"How could you boys possibly take me to the ball?"

"Never mind how," said Dawn. "Is it a deal?"

Mollyanna sniffed and shrugged. "All right then. It's a deal."

Eight

"No!" said Marcus.

"What do you mean, no?"

"N-O, no. No way!"

"You've got to do it," Dawn said. "Taking young Mollyanna to the ball is the only way you can get there yourself and find out what happened with the flute. It's not as if *I* could do it. I'm too young now, and by the time I'm old enough, I'd look too much like a girl."

The air was stifling in the cornfield. Tassels waved high above their heads, and all around them cicadas rasped with a rhythmic pulse that made the day seem hotter. So far there was no sign of the Removers van.

"Look at it this way," Dawn said. "You'll be twenty-two, and you'll be dying to take a girl to a dance. I bet Mollyanna—young Mollyanna, I mean—has grown a whole lot prettier. In 1922 she'd be fifteen."

"I don't know how to dance," Marcus muttered gloomily.

"You will. It's not you in 1986, remember. It's you in 1999."

Dawn sighed with relief when she spotted the van at last, parked in a bare patch in the middle of the field.

"Quick, we need you!" she called, pushing through the last row of corn.

Mr. Bros pulled a red bandanna from his pocket and wiped his brow. "You're a sight!" he commented, looking the children up and down with distaste. "What is it now?"

"We need to go forward this time," Dawn said breathlessly. "We need to go to 1999 and bring back Marcus when he's twenty-two so he can take Mollyanna to the Elmbridge Academy Senior Summer Ball."

"You do, do you?" Mr. Bros raised an eyebrow. "Why?"

"Dawn thinks I'll find out more about the flute," Marcus grumbled. "Personally, I think the idea stinks."

"For once I agree with you," said Mr. Bros. "Besides, it's against the rules. Can't bring things with you. Remember?"

"This isn't a thing, it's a person."

"Even worse. Sorry."

"But it's not just any person, it's Marcus," Dawn argued. "The same Marcus as now, only older. And Marcus has the coupon."

"What Marcus has is a genius for unnecessary complications," said Mr. Bros.

"Can you think of a simpler way?" Dawn asked.

"Of course, but I'm not allowed to help. It's against our policy. We remove you. Aside from that, you do the work."

"To 1999 then," said Dawn, "and could you stick around, please? We'll only be a minute."

"Have it your own way," said Mr. Bros. "I warn you, though, you won't like what you see."

Dawn had expected to see strange architecture, bizarre fashions, maybe even spaceships. Instead she saw her own living room in Weston, Massachusetts. The slipcovers on the armchairs had been changed, and there was a new television set with a much larger screen. Otherwise the room looked about the same. Sitting in the chairs were two persons who she realized, with sinking heart, must be themselves.

Grown-up Dawn had slung one leg over the arm of her chair and was watching television. Besides growing taller, she had put on weight. Her cheeks were puffy, and her thighs bulged in tight-fitting jeans. She was eating peanuts.

As for Marcus, he was handsome at the age of twenty-two, and judging by the conceited look on his face, he knew it. To Dawn's surprise he wore a tuxedo with a pink carnation pinned to the lapel. He sat slumped in his chair like a rag doll, holding a beer.

"Change the channel!" he ordered grown-up Dawn.

"Change it yourself."

"You could use the exercise," he told his sister. "Nothing more fattening than watching the soaps."

Grown-up Dawn scooped a handful of peanuts from the bowl and flung them at him.

"Watch it!" he snapped. "I have to take this monkey suit back to the rental place in the morning. If they charge me for grease spots, I'll tell them to send you the bill."

"And I'll tell them where they can stuff it," Dawn said, calmly stuffing her own mouth with peanuts. "Aren't you going to be late?"

"Who cares?" Marcus slumped down even farther in his chair. "Why did I let myself in for this? Escorting some pimply-faced debutante that I've never even met to a fund-raiser—a hundred dollars a plate, and what do you want to bet there's no booze? I've got to be out of my mind!"

"If you've never met her, how do you know she's pimply?" grown-up Dawn asked, her cheeks bulging. "Besides, her father paid for the tickets, so what are you complaining about?"

At this point Dawn stepped forward. She was horrified by grown-up Dawn, and she thought grown-up Marcus was a creep, but Mr. Bros was waiting.

"I've got a better idea," she said. "Want to get out of it? I'll take you to a classy, old-fashioned ball with a beautiful brunette. No pimples, I guarantee, and you won't have to pay a cent."

Grown-up Dawn jumped, scattering nuts across the floor. Grown-up Marcus kept his cool. He took a sip of beer and made the kind of face that grown-ups make to let children know they are not being cute. "Who let *you* in?"

"What do you want to bet it's Girl Scout cookies?" grown-up Dawn drawled. "What flavors are you selling, kids?"

"You need cookies like a hole in the head," her brother informed her. "Don't you ever look in the mirror?"

"I never get a chance. With Romeo in the house, all the mirrors are monopolized."

Dawn sighed. Would they ever stop bickering so that she and Marcus could get back to the ball? "We're not selling cookies. We came with an invitation. How about it?"

100

Grown-up Marcus eyed her suspiciously. "What's this, some kind of joke?"

"Of course not," said Dawn. "I'm perfectly serious. But I'm in a hurry too, so decide."

He laughed. "Come on, tell the truth. Whose idea was it? I have to admit, they did a fantastic job. You're perfect, both of you."

"Perfect what? What are you talking about?" For the first time, grown-up Dawn stared closely at the children. "My God, he's right—it's positively spooky!"

Hoisting herself from the armchair, she shuffled to the bookshelf, pulled out a photograph album, and flipped it open. "Here, take a look."

Dawn and Marcus saw two snapshots of themselves. In one they were standing on Uncle Doo's front step between their parents. In the other they sat on the same step next to Uncle Doo. Underneath was printed: "Christmas Eve, 1986."

"That was tomorrow," Dawn observed. "It's going to be a nice day."

"Very funny," said grown-up Dawn. "Now tell us who put you up to it."

"Nobody," Marcus said. "We're real."

"They must come from an actors' agency," grown-up Marcus told his sister. "Their voices are good, and the makeup is the work of a genius."

It had never occurred to Dawn that they might be recognized. But if their grown-up selves recognized Dawn and Marcus, surely they must know why they were there!

"We're not actors, we're you," she said excitedly. "I mean, you're us. Don't you remember? That Christmas in the photo, we kept traveling back and forth in time."

"You're wrong about the actors' agency," grown-up Dawn told her brother. "They're from a mental institution."

101

Dawn gave up. "Forget it. But it's true about the ball, I swear. Are you coming?"

"No," said grown-up Marcus. "Go away, both of you. I live with a bunch of freaks as it is, and I don't need two more."

For a moment Dawn forgot her errand. Who lived in that house in 1999? Were her parents still alive? Did she and Marcus have younger brothers and sisters? "What freaks?" she demanded. "What are their names?"

Grown-up Marcus smiled unpleasantly. "First there's skinny over there, with the peanuts," he told the children. "The other three are called Elroy, Liz, and Harry."

Marcus gasped. "Mom and Dad? I mean *your* mom and dad? You call them by their first names?"

"Never mind that," Dawn said hurriedly. "Who's Elroy?"

"You know what?" grown-up Marcus said to grown-up Dawn. "These aren't kids, these are midget agents of the C.I.A.!"

"Oh, please!" said Dawn. "Who is Elroy?"

"Elroy Doolittle, the eighth wonder of the world," said grown-up Dawn. "Ninety-four years old, and still going strong. When people get that old, they should do their families a favor and quietly pass away."

Dawn hated her more than ever. She wished she could run up and slap her face. Instead she took a deep breath. "Does he still play the flute?"

The older Dawn and Marcus both burst out laughing. "The flute? Elroy? Are you kidding?"

Dawn lost her temper. "I think you're disgusting, both of you. Don't you even care?"

She could see that it was useless. They not only didn't care, they had no idea what there could be to care about.

"Tell me one thing," she asked her grown-up self. "Are you a ballerina?"

The only answer was a chuckle from grown-up Marcus.

"Maybe you play the flute," Dawn continued hopefully. "Are you a famous flutist?"

This time grown-up Dawn laughed too.

"Oh, give up!" said Marcus. "Is he coming or not? Personally, I hope he doesn't. He's bad news."

But Dawn was stubborn. "Water ballet?" she asked. "Or did you decide to be a famous animal trainer?"

Before she could think of another question, a door opened behind her. Spinning around she caught sight of someone fairly familiar—no, someone *very* familiar. It was Liz Foster, her own mother. But this Liz Foster looked smaller, and her face was sad. And when this Liz Foster saw Dawn, she screamed.

"Cool it, Liz!" Grown-up Marcus stood up, brushed the peanuts from his tuxedo, and headed for the door. "I never did like practical jokes," he announced. "I'll take a chance on the fund-raiser."

The children followed, but Marcus lingered at the door. "Never mind him!" he told his future mother. "Never mind either of them. That's not what we're really like, and we'll prove it to you."

Dawn's cheeks burned with humiliation as she hurried after the tall figure in the tuxedo. "What did you say that for?" she asked her brother. "You just made things worse."

"I couldn't help it," Marcus said. "I hate that guy!"

"Then you hate yourself."

"It's not me. Let's call him something else."

"Like what?" Dawn asked.

"Like fathead."

Dawn shook her head. "If we insult him, we don't stand a chance. Do you want Uncle Doo to turn into a ninety-four-year-old man no one likes and who still can't play the flute?"

"I guess we could call him Marcus Two," Marcus conceded. "But if this doesn't work, it's all your fault."

Dawn was too upset to argue. The picture of her future mother wouldn't leave her mind as she followed Marcus Two along the streets of Weston. Liz had seemed so small, so bewildered, that Dawn felt like her mother's mother instead of her mother's daughter. She tried not to think about her grown-up self, but that face wouldn't leave her mind either.

"No one looked happy," Dawn muttered.

She concentrated on the changes in the neighborhood. Lots of the big elms were gone, and the fire hydrants had been replaced by squat, shiny cylinders, painted blue. Almost all the street crossings had over- or underpasses, and cars looked different, although not so different as she had expected. There were solar heating panels on every roof. Most of the houses were familiar, however. Dawn couldn't help wondering what had become of the families who used to live in them.

"Look!" she said. "There's Wendy Fulenwider's house. Do you think she still lives there?"

Marcus didn't answer. He shrugged and walked a little faster.

"Oh, cheer up!" said Dawn. "That wasn't our real mom. The real one is in Key West, having the time of her life."

Marcus looked at her pityingly. "Don't act stupid. This one was real too. But it's Uncle Doo I was thinking about. If he never played the flute, what are we doing this for? It proves we failed, back in 1986."

Dawn frowned, trying to figure it out. "I'm not so sure. It's odd how the grown-up *us* didn't remember anything about having been time travelers. It's as if it had never happened. But maybe it works both ways, and we could still change things so this future never happens."

104

"Whatever we do, we'd better do it fast," said Marcus. "Otherwise he'll go to that fund-raiser instead of the ball."

Marcus Two had turned into a narrow walkway leading to a house. Before the children could stop him, he knocked on the front door.

"Don't!" Dawn gasped, grabbing his elbow. "You'd have so much more fun with us!"

Marcus Two shook her off and smoothed his hair. "Run on home, kiddies. This ceases to amuse."

The door opened. His face twisted into a polite expression, but an instant later it switched to dismay. The young woman who stood before him in a long, green gown had not only pimples, but braces too.

Marcus Two bowed and turned away. "So sorry," he called over his shoulder. "Wrong address."

Shoulder to shoulder, the two children blocked the narrow walkway.

"That was mean!" said Marcus.

"It sure was," Dawn agreed, "but that's beside the point. It's a pity to rent a tuxedo and not use it. Come to the ball! What do you have to lose?"

"My temper," said Marcus Two, "if you brats don't disappear."

"You might meet the love of your life!" Dawn suggested without much conviction.

"You'll get to travel in space and time!" Marcus added daringly.

Pushing past them, Marcus Two strode down the walkway and crossed the street. Dawn stood with her brother, not knowing what to do. Was it worth following him? Even if they persuaded him to come, would he take one look at Mollyanna and leave again?

"Dawnie, look!" Marcus pointed at Marcus Two. "See that building behind him?"

It was a warehouse built of ugly cinderblock. Painted across its windowless facade in three-foot letters was: *20th CENTURY BROS REMOVERS—LFT 1999—Your Heart's Desire.* The van was parked in front.

"Stop!" Dawn yelled at Marcus Two. "You stop right there, you jerk, or you'll regret it all your life!"

Shocked into obedience, Marcus Two stopped short while Dawn and her brother crossed the street to where Mr. Bros, in shirt sleeves, was cleaning the windows of his cab.

"What does 'LFT' stand for?" Marcus asked.

"Latest Finishing Time, of course." Mr. Bros dipped a rag into a bucket of soapy water and scrubbed at the windshield without so much as a glance at the children.

"Is this your present then?" asked Dawn. "I mean, is your time now, so you only go back into the past?"

"My past. Other people's futures."

Dawn wondered if she would ever understand. "Is this your warehouse? What do you keep in it?"

Mr. Bros straightened up, wrung out his rag, and smiled. "What do I keep in it? A bunch of fools, that's what I keep in it. Only the one-way trippers, mind you—the ones who can't go home."

Dawn stared at the high, windowless walls. "In there? But there's no air, no light—and they're all alone!"

"They have each other, and that's more than they deserve," he told her. "They're the ones whose Hearts' Desires didn't make anyone happy but themselves."

Dawn imagined herself dancing or playing her singing flute forever behind those walls, and shuddered. "It's no fair!" she cried. "It's cruel, and it's probably unconstitutional, and I don't even want to think about it. We want to go back to 1922, and this creep is coming with us."

106

Mr. Bros gazed mockingly from her to Marcus Two. "Your wish is my command."

Carrying the bucket to the side, he climbed into the cab, started the motor, and moved the van.

Nine

They were in trouble from the start. Marcus Two was not happy to find himself wearing a tuxedo in the middle of a cornfield. Even the children thought it was unfair. Why couldn't Mr. Bros have put them closer to the gazebo? If this was his idea of a joke, it wasn't funny.

Although the sun was lower in the sky, the day was hotter than ever. Marcus Two removed his bow tie and unbuttoned his collar, but he was sweating so much that Dawn was afraid he would spoil his tuxedo before the ball had started.

"What happened?" he kept asking. "How the hell did I end up in a place like this?"

"I'm afraid I can't explain," said Dawn. "We don't understand ourselves, but we think it has to do with time warps."

Marcus Two removed a lavender silk cummerbund and pulled his crumpled shirttails loose. "Time warps! If anything is warped, it's your minds. Did you drug me or something?"

"Absolutely not," said Dawn. "I promise."

He shook his head in disbelief. "Listen, let's forget this classy ball business. Maybe I'll go to that fund-raiser after all."

Marcus gave Dawn a scornful glance. "I told you it was a dumb idea."

It was cooler when they reached the shelter of the gazebo, but Mollyanna was gone. In the middle of the floor she had left a covered basket, with a note on top.

" 'The ball begins at eight o'clock,' " Marcus read aloud. " 'I managed to sneak some food out of the Doolittles' kitchen. Help yourselves, and meet me at the Academy gates. *Bon appétit!*' "

On the back of the note was a hastily sketched map, showing that to reach the Academy they should turn left at the bottom of the driveway and continue for a mile and a half, once they had passed the pond.

"Are you kidding?" Marcus Two wiped his brow with a crumpled handkerchief. "I end up in a cornfield. God knows how, but it's too late to complain. Then you haul me off to this shack, and as if that's not enough, you tell me I have to walk another couple of miles before I get to the ball. What's it all about, can you tell me that?"

"No," said Marcus.

"Why not?" said Dawn. "Let's tell him the truth and see if he can help. After all, he's got your brains, plus thirteen years' more education."

Both Marcuses stared at her as if she had gone crazy.

109

"Here goes," Dawn continued. "Our great-uncle—who happens to be your great-uncle too, believe it or not— always wished he could play the flute. Because of this time warp thing, we can make that come true. But so far we've kind of messed it up. We wanted to find out why he stopped playing back in 1922, and the only way to do it was to borrow you out of the future, so you could take this friend of ours to a ball, so she could find out for us. Satisfied?"

"No," said Marcus Two. "Think of a better one."

"It's the truth, I swear," Dawn told him.

"If it's the truth, which I seriously doubt, why go to so much trouble spying around? Why not just ask your great-uncle?"

Dawn suspected he was right. If she and Marcus had found out a little more from Uncle Doo himself, maybe they could have avoided all those trips into the past. But it hadn't occurred to her. In fact, she realized, it hadn't occurred to her to chat with Uncle Doo at all, since she had arrived in Sunset Grove.

Marcus Two ate some cold chicken and drained the bottle of cider that Mollyanna had thoughtfully provided, but after treating the children to every four-letter word he could think of, he sat sulking in a corner.

"She'd better be worth it!" he muttered from time to time. "She'd better be gorgeous!"

She was not. When Dawn spotted her, standing next to grown-up Mollyanna at the Academy gates, her heart sank. She had powdered her face and painted her mouth with a vivid slash of lipstick. But Mollyanna, at fifteen, didn't look a day older than twelve-year-old Dawn. She was still skinny, her freckles showed through the powder, and her hair hung limply behind her ears. Dawn knew her gown would have looked sensational on someone else. It shimmered, and

110

was cut low both in front and in back. All the décolletage revealed, however, was more freckles, and bones.

She looked frightened, but her face lit up when she saw the children. "Don and Martin! You haven't changed a bit. Where have you been, all these years?"

"We'll tell you another time," said Dawn. "You'd better hurry now, or you'll be late for the ball. This is your date. He's really anxious to go in and dance."

Marcus Two backed away politely. "No hurry. I can see you're old friends. Why don't you go in together? Come to think of it, I have a previous engagement."

Dawn pulled him aside. "Listen," she whispered. "I know I can't force you to go to the ball, but I won't take you home until it's over. So which do you prefer—to wait here at the gates, or take her inside?"

He gave her a dirty look, took young Mollyanna by the elbow, and propelled her up the Academy drive.

"At least the refreshments will be good," Dawn said optimistically, watching them disappear into a brightly lit gymnasium. "Lucky them—caviar and champagne!"

Grown-up Mollyanna's eyes widened with surprise. "Champagne? Punch and cookies is more likely."

"Marcus Two doesn't strike me as the punch-and-cookies type," said Dawn. "He's going to need a couple of beers to get through the evening."

Mollyanna laughed. "This is 1922, remember? Prohibition. You can't buy alcohol at all, let alone serve it in a boys' school."

"Forget the beer," said Dawn. "We've got bigger problems. How are we going to get in there?"

"Who needs to go in?" asked Mollyanna. "All we have to do is wait. When Elroy sees young Mollyanna in her silver lamé gown, he'll forget he ever knew that silly Lillian

111

Prendergast. She'll twirl around the dance floor in the arms of the mysterious stranger and Elroy will go mad with jealousy. Her voice will rise in a delightful trill of laughter, she'll throw her head back and show her delicate neck—"

"I don't know what you've been reading," Dawn interrupted, "but it seemed to me that Marcus Two wanted to *wring* her delicate neck, and unless Lillian Prendergast has green hair and a long nose, Elroy isn't even going to notice young Mollyanna is alive. You've got to admit you look much better now."

"Besides, I hate to disappoint you," Marcus added, "but that Marcus Two isn't really me."

"Oh, yes he is," Dawn said sadly.

"He isn't," said Marcus. "He *may* be what I'll be someday, but he isn't me now. I can't see what he's seeing and I can't think what he's thinking, so how are we going to find out about Elroy and the flute? You made a deal, remember!"

Mollyanna's face fell. "You're right. Come with me."

She led them through a back door, into a pantry where servants in white aprons were bustling to and fro with trays. On a shelf near the door were more trays, and a stack of clean aprons. Following Mollyanna's example, the children each slipped on an apron, grabbed a tray, and walked into the ballroom with such self-assurance that no one questioned them.

"There they are!" said Mollyanna, pointing. "That stuck-up blonde dancing with Elroy is Lillian Prendergast, and oh, dear—there I am, standing over by the window."

Dawn observed young Mollyanna with growing pity. She was nervously fussing with the straps of her gown and making small talk, but it was clear that Marcus Two didn't

112

hear a word she said. His eyes were on Lillian Prendergast. Stuck-up or not, Lillian was the prettiest girl in the room.

"I hate to say this," Dawn whispered to grown-up Mollyanna, "but if anyone twirls around the dance floor, it'll be her, not you."

Elroy had slimmed down by the age of sixteen. Dawn thought he looked nice—much nicer than Marcus Two. But like Marcus Two, he was fascinated by Lillian. He stared into her eyes with a dazed expression, his mouth hanging open as if his mind had gone off in a hurry and forgotten to shut it. Dawn found herself blushing for him.

"There's nothing to her!" Mollyanna answered crossly. "Believe me, she's a complete nitwit, and I happen to know she bites her nails."

Dawn thought of her own bitten nails and hid her hands behind her back. "Well, we've done all we can for the time being. You stick with Marcus Two and make sure he doesn't get into trouble. I'll see if I can get closer to Elroy and find out about the flute."

She returned to the pantry and filled her tray with little sausages wrapped in bacon, each skewered with a toothpick. Then, skillfully avoiding anyone who tried to help himself, she slipped through the crowd. It took some time to find Lillian and Elroy; they had stopped dancing and had moved out to the terrace.

"Want any food?" she asked, thrusting the tray under Lillian's nose.

Lillian shrieked and pulled her skirts about her. "Take those nasty things away—they're greasy!"

"Just a minute!" said Elroy. His hand shot out.

Lillian gave an exaggerated shudder. "Ugh—how can you? Don't you dare spill a crumb on me!"

Elroy smiled apologetically. "Wouldn't dream of spoil-

113

ing your lovely gown," he mumbled with his mouth full.

"Really, darling!" said Lillian. "Sausage at a ball? I'll have to cure you of your plebeian tastes."

Elroy swallowed and smiled again. "Cure me of anything you like. My pleasure."

Lillian beamed at him and draped her arms around his neck. "Do you mean that, darling? Anything I like?"

"Anything at all," Elroy said rashly. "My word of honor."

Dawn groaned and nearly dropped her tray. How could he be so dumb? It was obvious that Lillian had something up her sleeve. No one with a brain in his head would trust her for a moment.

As if she could read Dawn's thoughts, Lillian swung around and glared. "Beat it, junior! Take your sausages elsewhere."

Dawn fled to the pantry and exchanged her tray for a plate of stuffed prunes. "She's no nitwit," she said to grown-up Mollyanna on her way back to the terrace, "but I admit, she's awful!"

Approaching the couple a second time, she caught the tail end of a sentence.

"—assure you, really quite pleasant, at the appropriate moment," Elroy was explaining.

"Certainly," Lillian said in a scornful voice. "In the evening after dinner, on the phonograph. But not onstage. Truly, darling, if you could see yourself you'd never play the flute again. Your lower lip sticks out in such a silly pout, and you grow seven double chins. Believe me, it's embarrassing!"

Elroy looked surprised. "Really? Of course, I've never practiced in front of a mirror."

"Really and truly." Lillian patted him coyly on the cheek. "I'm only telling you because I adore you. You know that,

114

don't you, darling? But you do look such a clown! And you wouldn't want poor little Lillian to be dancing with a clown, would you?"

Dawn was so angry that she heaved the plateful of prunes at poor little Lillian. "Don't listen to her, you fool!" she shouted. "Do you hear me, Elroy? Don't you *dare* give up that flute!"

There was a moment of stunned silence, during which Dawn was afraid that either Elroy or Lillian would murder her on the spot. Then a small form emerged from the shadows, with a taller form in tow. They were Marcus and Marcus Two.

From then on, Elroy didn't stand a chance. Marcus Two soothed, flattered, and consoled Lillian Prendergast, dabbing at her gown with a clean white handkerchief and finally leading her away.

"It was bound to happen," Marcus said gloomily. "He spotted her the minute he walked in. *All* the men were looking at Lillian. I don't think Elroy even noticed Mollyanna was at the ball."

"Maybe he'll notice now," said Dawn.

She was right. Young Mollyanna finally caught Elroy's attention and enticed him into a corner, where they shared a tray of food. From then on the evening went smoothly. Lillian Prendergast danced every dance with Marcus Two. Dawn noticed that her voice rose in a trill of laughter as she threw her head back and showed her delicate neck, but neither of the Mollyannas seemed to care. Dawn became sleepier and sleepier as she grew more and more bored.

"We can't do anything more," she said. "With luck, after the way Lillian treated him, Elroy will give up on her and go back to playing that flute. Let's leave."

115

But they couldn't leave, because Marcus Two had disappeared. They searched for him everywhere: weaving among the dancers, peering into every shadow on the terrace, behind every bush on the lawn. They startled a number of angry couples, but saw no signs of Lillian Prendergast and Marcus Two.

"Forget it," said Dawn. "Who cares? Let's go home anyway."

"But we can't!" Marcus wailed. "If I don't get me back to 1999, maybe I'll never grow up!"

Dawn glanced at him dubiously. "Do you want to grow up to be him?"

"Of course not," said Marcus. "Would you want to grow up to be his sister? But they're better than not growing up at all."

Dawn thought about her grown-up self. "She didn't do anything. Not ballet, or the flute, or anything at all. I wonder why."

Marcus shrugged. "Maybe she didn't practice. What I want to know is, how did I get to be so conceited?"

"From looking at yourself in the mirror, maybe," Dawn suggested.

She looked at her younger brother. His hair was rumpled and his face was smudged. A thought came to her. "We don't have to be like them! We've already changed a whole bunch of stuff in the past. It ought to be even easier to change things in the future."

"Maybe," Marcus said gloomily, "but that would be our own Heart's Desire."

They waited. The crowd grew thinner. Plates and glasses were collected, and the lights were put out in the pantry. At last the music stopped. Elroy left, escorting the young Mollyanna. Even grown-up Mollyanna slipped away, look-

116

ing more cheerful. Dawn and Marcus sat alone on the terrace until the stars faded and the sky warmed into a hazy, pink glow. They were both asleep when Marcus Two lurched into sight, his bow tie dangling from a jacket pocket and lipstick on his face.

"Misjudged you two," he told them in a voice so slurred that Dawn wondered if Mollyanna had been right about Prohibition. "Had a good time—sure beats fun-raising. Now less—less go home."

"That's fine with us," said Dawn. "You didn't happen to see a truck parked anywhere around, did you?"

"No. Less go look for one. Less ask 'em for a ride."

"Yes, less," said Marcus. He took his future self firmly by the elbow and steered him toward the Academy gate.

It was a long walk back to the cornfield.

They woke up the next morning to the sound of a flute. Marcus slipped out of bed and ran into the living room, only to come back with a disgusted look on his face.

"It's the radio."

Uncle Doo was fussing around the kitchenette, pulling packages from the freezer and squinting at the cooking instructions.

"Feeling rested?" he asked the children. "You were both dead to the world when I got home last night."

"We were kind of tired," Dawn admitted.

"I gathered as much. How about setting the table? Since it's Christmas Eve, I thought we might have something special. Make a change from Grape-Nuts."

Dawn set three places and picked flowers from Uncle Doo's garden to put in a jelly glass. When she had finished, there was still no smell of food, and Uncle Doo was still squinting at the packages with Marcus at his side.

117

"You take the plastic cover off before you put it in the oven," Marcus was saying. "The other way is only if you have a microwave."

Dawn's stomach rumbled. "Can I help?"

"Too many cooks spoil the broth," said Uncle Doo. "How about giving the house a sweep? With the broom, please. Don't fool with the Hoover."

Dawn sighed and reached for the broom. She did the halls quickly before tackling her bedroom where, in spite of Uncle Doo's warnings, she and Marcus had tracked in sand. After that she did Uncle Doo's room, and while she was at it, she took a good look at the flute. It looked exactly like her own flute that she had jammed under the backseat of the car, except that it didn't look used. The pads under the keys were cracked. The tiny springs and hinges were crusted with greasy dust that wouldn't wipe off. This flute had not been played for years. Dawn didn't know whether to be angry or to cry. For this they had stayed up all night, gone to so much trouble?

"It doesn't look as if he's practiced much lately," Marcus said, coming in to tell her the food was ready.

"Mastermind at work!" said Dawn. "How did you reach your brilliant conclusion?"

She followed Marcus to the table, but she had lost her appetite.

Uncle Doo's idea of a special breakfast was frozen waffles, frozen scrambled eggs with sausage, frozen cinnamon donuts, and frozen orange juice. In spite of having been in the oven, much of it was still frozen. There was no maple syrup for the waffles, so he served them with grape jelly.

Dawn wondered whether Uncle Doo's feelings would be hurt if she scraped her plate into the sink and had a bowl of Grape-Nuts instead. She took a sip of juice and thought wistfully of the acres of orchards she had noticed while driving across the state.

"You'd think that in Florida, people would squeeze their own juice!" she said crossly.

"Some do."

"Why don't you, then? If you like orange juice, why don't you make it fresh?"

"Too much trouble," said Uncle Doo, calmly pouring himself another glass.

Too much trouble. Dawn wondered if that hadn't been the problem all along, ever since the days that Uncle Doo was Elroy. He was easygoing, unresisting, quietly pursuing his private dream—as long as it wasn't too much trouble— yet filled with bitter disappointment. The thought made her crosser than ever.

"Frozen food stinks! It isn't even good for you—didn't anyone ever tell you that? It's got too many additives. And while we're on the subject, how come you don't play that flute?"

Marcus gasped. Even Uncle Doo was startled out of his usual mild composure.

"What subject?" he demanded.

Dawn was silent. She wished she hadn't opened her mouth.

"I used to play it, years ago," Uncle Doo said, after a moment's thought. "One of these days I ought to find out where to get it overhauled. Nice instrument. Made in France, close to a century ago."

"How long did you play it?" Marcus asked. "When did you give it up?"

Uncle Doo pushed his chair back and began clearing the dishes. "Let's see. I started lessons when I was a little younger than you, Dawn. Got pretty good at it, too. I played at school, in the marching band. Didn't like that much. Kept tripping over my own feet. Orchestra was more my cup of tea. I hoped to join the orchestra when I went to Harvard, but I never made it. That's about when I stopped playing."

"Harvard University?" Dawn did some mental arithmetic. "When would that have been, 1922?"

" 'Twenty-four," said Uncle Doo. "I didn't get around to auditioning until fall of junior year. Didn't audition at all, come to think of it."

Marcus wriggled with impatience. "What do you mean, you didn't? If you didn't even audition, how do you know you never made it?"

"Missed the audition," said Uncle Doo, and he carried the plates out to the kitchenette.

"Are you sure it's really his Heart's Desire?"

Marcus's voice was muffled: He was half hidden in the suitcase, looking for a clean white shirt. Uncle Doo had invited Kelly and Lisa for the morning. He was taking them all to the library for a Christmas party.

"It was your idea, not mine," Dawn said, straining her arms to fasten the buttons at the back of her dress. "You had the coupon, and you used it for Uncle Doo."

"I know, and I don't mind, because who wants to end up in a warehouse in 1999? But what's the point, if it isn't his real Heart's Desire? We should have chosen someone else's."

Dawn thought about it. It struck her that she didn't know much about other people's Hearts' Desires. What did her mother or father secretly long for, or her friends at school? Come to think of it, did she even know about herself? She had daydreams, but did she care enough to help make them come true? Was she like Elroy?

"Hurry up and get dressed," she said to change the subject.

"I don't have a clean white shirt. I don't even have a clean T-shirt, and all my underwear is dirty too. It's a good thing Mom and Dad are coming back this afternoon."

"This afternoon?" Dawn was suddenly struck by reality. "That's not a good thing, it's terrible! We've only got half a day left, and we're still in 1924. How many times are we going to have to go back and rescue that idiot? Can't he understand that if you want something badly enough, you have to make an effort to get it?"

Marcus grinned. "Preach, preach, preach! I thought you hated preaching. Maybe Elroy hates preaching too."

"It's probably the only thing we have in common," Dawn said. "That's maybe why I'm the only person who can help him."

"You?" Marcus glared indignantly. "Who got the coupon in the first place? Who remembered Uncle Doo's Heart's Desire? Who thought of asking Mr. Bros to pick where we should go?"

"You did," Dawn said. "Don't get so upset—I was only joking."

Marcus chose a shirt that looked cleaner than the others, although it had ketchup on the cuffs. "You know what, Dawnie? You're no fun to fight with anymore."

121

Ten

Kelly and Lisa looked as if they had run out of clean clothes too. Their dresses were stained with chocolate, orange juice, and something green that Dawn guessed was either pistachio ice cream or grass.

Marcus's face was so unwelcoming that Dawn made an effort in spite of herself to be friendly. "Do you live here?"

"Are you crazy?" said Kelly. "We're from Baltimore. We just got sent here over Christmas, because my mom's having another baby. I hope it's a boy; I couldn't stand another Lisa."

Dawn glanced at Lisa, who was standing in front of Uncle Doo's T.V., switching channels so fast that she couldn't possibly recognize the programs in between. "Why? What's wrong with her?"

Kelly shrugged and looked bored. "Oh, you know. She thinks she's so cute. What do you want to do?"

"I don't think we have time for anything," said Dawn. "Uncle Doo is taking us to a party, isn't he?"

Kelly giggled. " 'Uncle Doo' is such a silly name. Besides, he's too old to be your uncle."

"He's my great-uncle, really," Dawn explained. "You see, my mother's mother—"

Kelly showed no interest in Dawn's mother's mother. She joined Lisa at the television set and fiddled with the knobs. "What's wrong with your T.V.? I can't get HBO."

"Uncle Doo doesn't have cable T.V."

Kelly opened her eyes wide. "You're kidding! What's the matter—can't he afford it?"

"I think he just doesn't care," said Dawn. "He never watches anything but classical music and news."

"You can't watch that," Kelly told her scornfully.

"What do you want to bet? He was watching the other night. It was an orchestra, playing something."

"Then he's weird," said Kelly. "My grandmother told me he's weird. She says your parents must be crazy to leave you alone with him, the way he lives by himself in this tacky cottage place and doesn't come to the condo meetings. She says she asked him three times to her Attitude Readjustment Hour, and he wasn't even polite when he said no."

Dawn tried to make sense of all this garbled information. "She asked him to her what?"

"Attitude Readjustment Hour," Kelly repeated. "That's a joke. It means happy hour. You know, all the senior cits

123

get together at five o'clock for Bloody Marys, and they play shuffleboard."

"I'd say no too," said Dawn.

Kelly switched to a channel where there was horse racing, and Lisa screamed.

"Turn it back! I was watching *Electric Company!*"

"So?" Kelly flopped down in a chair and stared at the screen.

"So turn it back. I got here first!"

"I'm the oldest."

"So you have to be nice to me. Mom said."

"Touch that button and I'll cream you!" Kelly threatened.

Lisa switched back to *Electric Company*. Kelly flung herself out of the chair, grabbed her sister by her pink-socked ankles, and threw her to the floor. On her way down Lisa fell against a table, knocking over two plastic houseplants.

Uncle Doo's bedroom door opened a crack. "Could you conceivably tone it down to a dull roar?"

"See?" Kelly said as the door shut again. "He's weird!"

Dawn and Marcus stood together by the window, watching silently.

"That Kelly is awful!" Marcus whispered. "She's so mean to Lisa."

"I can't understand why she acts that way," Dawn said. Then she thought back to Sunday morning. "Am I that bad?"

"You? Like Kelly? No way!"

"But you said, the other day. You said I was mean."

"Maybe you were," Marcus admitted, "but not so much lately."

"That was only three days ago."

"Well, you're different now."

124

Dawn felt a thrill of excitement. Had she changed? Were they both changing? Was it really possible to avoid becoming the Dawn and Marcus of 1999? She was on the point of asking Marcus what he thought about it, but felt suddenly embarrassed. It was almost a relief when Lisa ran up to her, howling over a drop of blood that had appeared on her knee.

Dawn led Lisa to the kitchenette, where Uncle Doo kept the first-aid kit. "It's only a scratch," she told her, applying ointment and a Band-Aid. She suspected that Lisa would be black and blue all over, the next day, but that was Kelly's problem. "Want a Coke or something?"

Lisa had stopped screaming when she realized there was no hope of punishing her older sister. "I want a milk shake," she said, wiping her nose on the back of her hand.

"This isn't McDonald's," said Dawn. "How am I supposed to make a milk shake?"

Kelly appeared in the doorway. "With ice cream and milk. How else?"

She threw open the freezer door and took out a pint of cherry swirl, which she emptied into Uncle Doo's blender, along with the last of the milk.

"Hey, wait a minute!" said Dawn. "I don't think we're supposed to use that thing. I don't think it works. Uncle Doo never—"

It was too late. Kelly plugged it in and pushed a button. Within two seconds the three girls, the counters, and the walls were coated with cherry swirl.

This time there was no scream. In dead silence Kelly led Lisa across the living room and out the front door. Dawn was left with the mess.

"I didn't have anything to do with it, you know," said Marcus.

125

Dawn wiped the counter with a sponge. "Who said you did?"

"Just so you don't tell Uncle Doo it was my fault. I wasn't even there. I hid behind the sofa."

"I noticed," said Dawn.

"I couldn't help it. She was scary. What makes her that way?"

Dawn sponged the cupboards over the sink. "I don't know. I'm not particularly interested."

"That's another way you're like Elroy, then," Marcus said. "He never seems particularly interested in anything. I bet he was never particularly interested in playing that flute, even. He never really cared."

Dawn wrung out her sponge and pretended not to hear, but she was troubled. Could Mr. Bros's coupon really help Uncle Doo? She knew she would never use it to get her own Heart's Desire. Like Marcus, she dreaded ending up in a warehouse in 1999. If she wanted something badly, she would have to get it by herself. But did she really care enough? Was she really like Elroy, and would she end up like Uncle Doo?

"If he doesn't care, I'll care *for* him," she told Marcus. "Let's try one more time."

"That's more like it!" Mr. Bros said approvingly when they mentioned 1924. "September is what you're looking for. The first Thursday in September."

His smile was so cheerful that Marcus asked him what was wrong. "Not that I mind," he added, "but up to now you've always looked as if we were the last people in the world you wanted to see."

"What do you expect?" asked Mr. Bros. "You didn't come by that coupon honestly, after all. Frankly, you weren't the type of person I would have given it to. But you seem to be wrapping things up nicely. With luck I'll have seen the last of you."

Dawn felt strangely disappointed. "Are we really that bad?"

"Not as bad as I thought," Mr. Bros conceded, "but a nuisance, all the same. You get an idea and you're hell-bent to carry it through before you think it out. No consideration for the persons concerned. What's it to you that I just got back from Monte Carlo, 1935, and I have to leave again for Moscow, 1989, without a moment to put my feet up and smoke a pipe? No, you have to be here, there, and everywhere, and all at your own convenience."

He drove away, leaving them on the bridge over the pond in the Boston Public Garden.

"Here?" cried Dawn. "But we come here all the time, back home in Massachusetts!"

"It looks like we *are* back home in Massachusetts," Marcus said. "The problem is when, and why?"

They soon found out. Leaning over the rail to look at a Swan Boat that was passing under the bridge, they recognized Elroy and Mollyanna.

It was a beautiful day, noticeably warmer than the day they had left in Sunset Grove. Leaves were turning. The air was crisp and smelled of autumn, but people were still strolling about in their summer clothes. Elroy wore a panama. Mollyanna was startlingly pretty in spite of her freckles and thinness. She had on a short, waistless dress and a little blue hat that brought out the blue sparkle in her eyes. Dawn decided it wasn't her clothes that were pretty, or her eyes, or anything else she could point to. It was the sparkle, and Elroy seemed to like it too.

127

"We're in the right place," she told Marcus. "They can't go anywhere before they get off at the dock. Let's just wait."

They waited for close to an hour. Each time the Swan Boat circled back to the dock, Elroy and Mollyanna produced another ticket and stayed on. They sat close together in the front seat, and Elroy's arm was casually draped over Mollyanna's shoulder.

"They're impossible!" Dawn stooped to scratch a mosquito bite on her ankle. "Isn't there a rule against staying on so long?"

"It isn't as if there were a line," said Marcus. "Maybe we ought to get on too."

They found just enough money in their pockets to pay the fare—an additional annoyance, as they would rather have spent it on pretzels. But, as Marcus pointed out, "Who knows if the pretzel cart was here in 1924?"

The Swan Boats were the same, with their rows of benches that looked as if they ought to be settled respectably along a path, rather than floating on the water. Except for clothes, not much had changed. The man in the Swan pedaled the boat the same way around the island, and children with almost familiar faces threw bread crusts to ancestors of the ducks Dawn and Marcus fed in 1986. But the girl children all wore dresses, the men wore hats, and the women wore shiny silk stockings that made even Mollyanna's legs look pink and plump.

"And the shoes!" Dawn said, pointing under the benches at various pairs of feet. "They're all so important-looking!"

Marcus agreed. "It feels more like Sunday than Thursday. Everyone looks dressed for church."

Elroy and Mollyanna were not on their way to church; they were discussing their plans for the evening.

"Let's just stay here," Mollyanna suggested dreamily. "Round and round the island, day and night, winter and summer, until we're white-haired and old."

"The boats don't run in winter," Elroy said. "It would be too damn cold."

Mollyanna smiled as if he had said something brilliant. "So it would, darling. I was just being silly."

"You're being adorable!" said Elroy, and he looked at her the way he had once looked at Lillian Prendergast.

Marcus made a sick face behind his back.

"Don't you think that's about enough now?" Elroy suggested as the boat drew near the dock.

"No," said Mollyanna.

Elroy pulled a gold watch from his pocket. "I know it's early for supper, but I have an audition tonight at eight."

Mollyanna laughed. "Supper? How can you think of eating at a time like this?"

"Oh, well . . ." Elroy was torn between romance and greed. "Got to feed that pretty little face," he said hopefully. "Can't let that pretty little body waste away!"

"It won't," said Mollyanna.

"The Ritz-Carlton is just across the street," said Elroy. "You can sit by the window and look down at the Public Garden. That's almost as good as being here, isn't it?"

"Only almost."

Elroy was beginning to look desperate, and the children sympathized. They couldn't afford to buy another ticket.

"How about the Parker House?" he said. "That's always a nice place for a lady."

Mollyanna made an unladylike sound. "Baked beans? If you try to feed me baked beans, I swear I *will* waste away, Elroy Doolittle!"

"How about baked oysters?" Elroy asked. "Baked oysters and sweetbreads under glass, upstairs at Locke-Ober's."

Mollyanna perked up. "That's more like it! What are we waiting for?"

Dawn and Marcus followed the couple down Tremont Street to Winter Place. It wasn't until they reached the restaurant that they were noticed. Mollyanna stopped to pull out her compact and a comb. Catching a glimpse of Marcus in the mirror, she spun around and cried out.

"Martin! What are you doing here? Why is Don dressed like a girl?"

"I'm afraid I *am* a girl," Dawn said with an embarrassed glance at the dress she had put on for the Christmas Eve party.

Mollyanna looked her up and down. "So you are. But why have you come back?"

"Don't you remember?" Marcus asked. "We made a deal."

"I don't understand," said Elroy. "Do you know these children?"

"Of course I do," Mollyanna told him impatiently. "So do you. They came to the gazebo, after your tenth birthday party."

Elroy smiled at her fondly. "Dearest, that was nine years ago. Those children would be grown up by now."

"Grown up?" Mollyanna's face clouded with confusion. "I suppose you're right, but they were at the ball, too, the summer you graduated. The same children, I assure you. I don't believe they grow."

"You're a darling!" said Elroy, tapping her affectionately on the tip of her nose. "A dear, whimsical darling. I'm going to take you inside and feed you baked oysters."

Mollyanna opened her compact a second time and powdered the tip of her nose. "Just so long as it isn't baked beans." She glanced suspiciously over her shoulder at the children as Elroy opened the door to Locke-Ober's and ushered her inside.

"Don't be late, Elroy!" Marcus yelled after them. "Don't forget, you have an audition at eight o'clock!"

"Dummy," said Dawn. "What good do you think that will do?"

"You never know. Maybe all he needed was to be reminded."

"Mollyanna ought to remind him herself," Dawn said crossly. "I thought she was on our side."

Marcus thought for a moment. "I don't think this is the same Mollyanna. The Mollyanna we met in the gazebo had a coupon, like us. Remember? And we made the deal with her. But young Mollyanna, the one Marcus Two took to the ball, didn't know anything about it. I think this is young Mollyanna, more grown up."

"Whichever it is, she has a one-track mind," said Dawn. "Can you imagine going to all that trouble just for Elroy?"

Marcus shrugged. "That's what *we're* doing, isn't it?"

"Not for Elroy," said Dawn. "For Uncle Doo."

Then she laughed. "Won't you be glad when this is over and there's only one of everybody again?"

Marcus nodded. "But it'll never be over if he stays in there all night eating oysters. I'm not leaving until I make sure he comes out on time."

"Baked oysters and sweetbreads under glass!" Dawn sighed as she settled herself for a long wait. "How do you suppose he ever ended up with a freezer full of fish sticks?"

The sun disappeared behind the buildings and the sky grew darker. Every half hour a bell tolled in the distance.

131

The time between the tollings seemed endless to the children.

"Seven-thirty," Marcus said finally, rising stiffly to his feet. "I'm going to drag him out."

Dawn was horrified. "Out of Locke-Ober's? They might call the police!"

"Who cares? What happens to us in 1924 doesn't matter, does it? I mean, we can't be really us."

"I feel like really me," said Dawn. "If a policeman came, I wouldn't know how to explain."

Luckily she didn't have to. The door swung open, and Elroy and Mollyanna stepped into the street. Mollyanna's eyes sparkled more than ever, but Elroy looked distressed. He stopped in the middle of Winter Street to study his pocket watch.

"Don't bother," Marcus said, moving out of the shadows. "It's half past seven. You'll just make it, if you hurry."

"Yes, please hurry!" Dawn begged. "You can't miss that audition. It's important. It might be a turning point in your life!"

Mollyanna looked surprised. "Is it really as important as all that? Well, I don't mind, but Elroy has to walk me home first."

"All the way out to the country?" cried Dawn. "It'll take forever."

"Of course not," Mollyanna said impatiently. "I'm boarding with a lady in Forest Hills. I study piano now, at the Conservatory."

Dawn groaned. "You've got to be joking. Forest Hills is miles away."

"Mollyanna likes to walk," Elroy informed them in a voice that lacked enthusiasm. "I can't let her walk home alone."

132

At the best of times, Dawn did not find it easy to keep her temper. Now she stopped trying. "You know what's going to happen if you walk Mollyanna home? You're going to turn into an eighty-one-year-old grouch who's a lousy cook, that's what."

Elroy opened his mouth and snapped it shut again. Then he opened it a second time. "Grouch?"

"Grouch," Dawn repeated firmly. "But if you go to that audition, you might just end up happy."

Elroy looked at his watch again, then back at Mollyanna. "It's not too late. Why don't you come along?"

"Come along where—to Harvard Yard? Most likely it'll be a place where they don't allow women."

"Most likely," Elroy agreed, "but you can wait for me outside. I'll only be a minute. Take you home afterward, in a cab."

"Wait outside?" Mollyanna stamped her foot. "Elroy Doolittle, do you care about me or don't you? Make up your mind! I love music too, but I don't put it above my friends."

Dawn took a deep breath and reminded herself that this wasn't the Mollyanna who had made the deal. "If you're really Elroy's friend, you'll let him go," she said. "Martin and I will walk you home."

It was a long, long way to Forest Hills. The children followed Mollyanna down Washington Street, block after endless block. She walked with the brisk step of someone who is offended, but too well bred to let it show. The children wondered how she kept up the pace in her fancy shoes. Their own feet ached and their legs felt weak by the time Mollyanna reached her lodgings.

"I didn't expect her to thank us, but she didn't even

133

say good night!" Dawn complained after Mollyanna had slammed the door in their faces.

"She was mad," Marcus said unnecessarily.

Dawn nodded. "I know. I guess she's in love with him. I wonder if she gets him in the end?"

"Of course she doesn't," Marcus said. "Uncle Doo never married, you know that."

"Unless that other Mollyanna makes herself his Heart's Desire," Dawn reminded him.

The thought was so funny that they laughed all the way back to the Boston Public Garden.

It was so late by the time they got there that most of the city lights were out, and the streets were empty. Even Mr. Bros was half asleep in the driver's seat. The children themselves were so tired that when Uncle Doo caught them standing by the sundial, they didn't have the strength to think up an excuse.

"I thought I told you not to fool with my garden," said Uncle Doo.

Dawn and Marcus stood still, forlornly nodding.

"What did I do to deserve this?" Uncle Doo sputtered as he led them back inside. "What have you been up to, in the last five minutes, for your clothes to be such a mess?"

Dawn hobbled to the living room where she sank down on the sofa and kicked off her shoes. "I'm sorry. I hope we didn't make you late for your party."

"I don't know what you're talking about," said Uncle Doo. "I'm late for my *rehearsal!*"

Rehearsal? Dawn caught her breath. Hardly daring to hope, she watched Uncle Doo dash into his bedroom and reappear with an instrument case and a sheaf of music. Then she let her breath out in a loud cheer.

"We did it! Marcus, we really did it—he plays the flute!"

134

In spite of her sore feet she jumped off the sofa, ran over to Uncle Doo, and hugged him so hard that he dropped the music.

Uncle Doo smiled as he retrieved the scattered sheets. "If I'm playing the flute tonight, it's no thanks to you, you little devils. I could hardly hear myself practice, with the television turned on high all week. How about finding something more imaginative to do for once?"

Eleven

The broadcast bells chimed ceaselessly all afternoon. Marcus, who was feeding the gulls, said the notes were like the white birds wheeling in the air above his head: thievish and greedy.

Dawn objected. "How can bells be greedy?"

She kept a safe distance. The gulls were beautiful in flight, but she couldn't bear their beady eyes and evil beaks up close.

"They're greedy because they keep wanting something from us," Marcus explained. "They want us to feel like Christmas, and I don't."

Dawn didn't either, in spite of the bells, and the styrofoam Santa in front of Sunset Arcade whose eight reindeer were harnessed to a speedboat rather than a sleigh. The Hawaiian-style bar outside the Holiday Inn was festooned with green and red crepe paper, and blinking light bulbs in the shape of angels. She tried to think of it as Miss Purvis did—a place more like Bethlehem than her hometown in Massachusetts. It didn't work.

"Look!" said Marcus. "There's Uncle Doo with that Miss Purvis."

The two old people sat at a table in the Hawaiian Bar. Miss Purvis had kicked off her shoes again, and was wiggling her toes in the sand. There was a piña colada on the table in front of her. Uncle Doo was drinking ginger ale.

"The rehearsal must be over," Dawn said. "Let's find out what happened."

Miss Purvis waved. "Sit down and have a drink. We're celebrating."

"Celebrating what?" Marcus asked, slipping into a chair beside her.

"Good rehearsal," said Uncle Doo. "We'll be sounding great tonight."

"You mean you're playing at the midnight service?" Dawn asked.

Miss Purvis beamed. "You children have never heard your great-uncle play, have you? He's very talented. The best flutist I ever accompanied. We're lucky to have him here in Sunset Grove."

Uncle Doo smiled modestly into his empty glass.

"Have another," Miss Purvis advised, pushing her chair back and rising to her feet. She trotted barefoot toward the bar and came back with a second ginger ale and two Cokes.

"But Miss Purvis," Marcus said, "if Uncle Doo is playing

137

at the church tonight, then he's the flutist that you said couldn't play worth a damn!"

She stared. "I couldn't have said that, dear. It wouldn't have been true."

Dawn kicked Marcus under the table, but he insisted. "You did too, that afternoon you stayed so late. You said the flutist couldn't play worth a damn, but Bach would survive."

Miss Purvis shook her head. "Impossible. After all, your great-uncle played for years with the Boston Symphony."

Marcus had barely opened his mouth to protest when Kelly walked by with her sister.

"Hello, Mr. Doolittle!" she said, stopping at their table. "You're playing at the church tonight, aren't you? My grandmother is letting us stay up for the service."

Before Uncle Doo could answer, Dawn asked, "Did you get the stains out of your dress?"

Kelly looked confused, but she held her hand out politely. "Hi! I'm Kelly Wilson. Is Mr. Doolittle your grandfather?"

"He's my great-uncle." Dawn corrected her, feeling dizzy. "You see, my mother's mother was his sister."

"Hey, that's neat!" said Kelly. "Is this your brother? Are you staying long? We're going to the video arcade. Want to come?"

Dawn couldn't believe it. Was Kelly acting, or was this something else they had changed by getting Uncle Doo his Heart's Desire? "Maybe we'll meet you there," she said. "Thanks for asking."

"What's the matter?" Marcus whispered. "They didn't recognize us!"

"No," said Dawn, "and I bet the cherry swirl is back where it was in Uncle Doo's freezer. What do you suppose we did in 1924 to change Kelly Wilson?"

"Uncle Doo had a rehearsal instead of that Christmas party," Marcus reasoned, "so I guess he just plain didn't invite them over."

"But we met them before that. We met them way back at the first concert, and Kelly was a real pain. Now she's nice."

"Maybe we changed things more than we meant to," Marcus said.

Dawn shivered. "I hope not. I hope it's just the flute, and Kelly, and the cherry swirl."

Marcus nodded, but his attention was elsewhere. "Look!"

He pointed over Miss Purvis's shoulder at a young woman who was sitting alone a few tables away. Unlike the other vacationers, she was not wearing a bathing suit, or even shorts. It was Mollyanna in a dress and high heels, and a little felt hat.

She was staring at Miss Purvis's back, and tears ran down her cheeks.

"What's wrong with her?" Marcus asked. "Which Mollyanna is it?"

"The one we made the deal with, of course. The other one didn't have a coupon." Dawn shoved back her chair and moved toward Mollyanna's table, but Mollyanna jumped up and ran away.

"Follow her!" Marcus called.

Dawn shook her head. "It's no use. I wish I knew why she was so unhappy, though. I have a horrible feeling it's our fault."

"Oh, come off it!" said Marcus, who had been counting the empty glasses on her table. "I bet she's just sorry she had four piña coladas."

The children went home, hoping to find Mollyanna waiting for them with an explanation, but the apartment was deserted. Only one thing had changed since they had left: As Dawn had predicted, the cherry swirl ice cream was back in the freezer.

Marcus's face expanded with a sudden surge of power. "We changed it!" he cried triumphantly. "First it happened, and then we made it unhappen again. I bet we could change anything we wanted, all over the twentieth century. We could unsink the *Titanic*! We could unerupt Mount Saint Helens, and save the spaceship *Challenger*!"

Dawn thought of the tears on Mollyanna's face. "I don't know," she said. "So far, we may have done as much harm as good."

"Come on, Dawn! We got Uncle Doo his Heart's Desire. Now we can have fun."

Dawn shook her head. "It wasn't fair. We made a deal with grown-up Mollyanna, and we didn't keep our part of it."

"She didn't either," Marcus pointed out. "Look how she tried to keep Elroy from going to his audition."

"That was young Mollyanna," said Dawn. "This one tried to help, and we let her down."

They turned the sundial several times, but they had a long wait before the van appeared. When it did, Mr. Bros looked so forbidding that Dawn wished she could run back into the house.

He was dressed in a top hat and a morning coat, all of the palest gray, with a white carnation in his buttonhole.

"This is beyond a joke," said Mr. Bros.

"It's not a joke at all," said Dawn. "Otherwise we wouldn't bother you. I know you're busy. Where are you off to now?"

"A wedding in Philadelphia. Your parents' wedding, as a matter of fact. Not that it's your business."

140

"That's nonsense!" Marcus told him flatly. "They're already married. Anyway, they're in Key West, not Philadelphia."

"They may be now," said Mr. Bros. "My appointment is in 1969."

Dawn gasped. "They're not even in Key West anymore. They're on their way to Sunset Grove, and they'll be here this afternoon. We have to hurry!"

Mr. Bros fixed her with a stern eye. "Haste makes waste."

Dawn paid no attention. "We have to go back one more time, for Mollyanna."

"No," said Mr. Bros.

"Why not? We won't take long."

"No," he repeated. "You're through. One Heart's Desire, ordered and delivered. There's a performance tonight, if I'm not mistaken."

Marcus shrugged and turned toward the house, but Dawn grabbed his sleeve. "Wait, Marcus."

She took a deep breath and tried to keep her voice steady. "I know we didn't earn the first coupon, but if you give us another I'd be willing to pay for it, no matter how much you charge. I probably can't afford it right away, but I'll work and pay you back, I promise. Only please, please let me help Mollyanna."

Marcus gave her a look of surprise which turned to admiration. "You don't have to say 'we' about the coupon, Dawnie. I took it from the van, not you. And if you want to earn another one, I'll help you."

Mr. Bros stared at them for a long time. Then he smiled. "I'll make an exception," he said, "but no more of this flitting back and forth. One round trip, and it's your only chance. Where to?"

Marcus stepped forward eagerly. "Forest Hills, 1924."

"No!" said Dawn. "It's no use trying to help *that* Mollyanna. She didn't know her own mind. Let's help the one who cared."

The Mollyanna who cared—the Mollyanna who bicycled into the pond, who met them in the gazebo before the ball, who wept over piña coladas in the Hawaiian Bar—still lived in Forest Hills, in 1942. She was sitting before a small upright piano, staring at the keyboard. Dawn guessed that they were in her bedroom. A cot in the corner had been disguised to look like a sofa, and various items of clothing hung from hooks and doorknobs, some still wet from recent laundering. Outside it was snowing.

"Winter," Marcus said aloud.

"It's Christmas Eve," Mollyanna murmured.

She turned and smiled. "You're back! And this time you've come to visit me, instead of the other way around."

"By the other way around, do you mean when you were in the bar on Sunset Beach this afternoon?" Dawn asked.

"Not this afternoon. That was at least a month ago."

"But you said today is Christmas Eve. When you came to Sunset Beach it was Christmas Eve for us, too."

"Perhaps," said Mollyanna, "but for me it was November. I haven't asked Mr. Bros to remove me at all since November."

Dawn tried to figure it out, but failed. "Why did you come? Why were you crying?"

Mollyanna twirled the piano stool so that she was facing them. "I was curious. I wanted to see your great-uncle. It was hard to believe that for you he's eighty-one years old. And I wanted to see what 1986 was like. I thought the bar was silly, but I adored the cocktail. I asked the man to give me the same thing the fat old lady was drinking. It was delicious!"

142

"If you mean Miss Purvis, it was a piña colada," said Dawn.

Mollyanna was already pale, but she turned a little paler. "Miss who?"

"Miss Anna Purvis. She plays the piano. She's Uncle Doo's accompanist."

"But he isn't married to her?"

"No way!" said Marcus.

"She didn't see me, did she?" Mollyanna asked.

"I don't think so," Dawn said. "She had her back to you."

Mollyanna sighed. "It's just as well. Poor thing—she was old and fat."

Dawn corrected her. "She's plump, not fat. Didn't anyone ever tell you that in every fat old lady there's a skinny little girl trying to get out?"

Mollyanna smiled the saddest smile Dawn had ever seen anyone smile. "Maybe I'm the skinny little girl trying to get *in*. I don't care if that old lady is fat and that your great-uncle is eighty-one years old. I'd like to be her, married to him."

"Except she isn't," Marcus reminded her.

Mollyanna sighed. "No, I can see she isn't. And I gather your great-uncle got his Heart's Desire. You said she was his accompanist. Does that mean he gives concerts?"

Dawn nodded. "He's playing at his church tonight."

It was dark in the room, in spite of a lamp near the piano. Dawn didn't think it could be nice to live there. Although Mollyanna had tried to cheer it up with pictures and ornaments, it looked like what it was: a small bed-sitting room in a cheap boardinghouse.

Dawn moved to the bedside table and picked up a china dog with a clock in its stomach. "This is cute! Listen, Mollyanna. We came back because you probably think Uncle Doo got the wrong Heart's Desire."

"No he didn't," said Marcus. "His Heart's Desire was playing the flute. Mollyanna's was to marry him."

Dawn glared at him. "The point is, we made a deal, so we came back to see if we could help."

Mollyanna closed the lid gently over the keyboard. "That's kind of you, but I gave up long ago. Last November, as a matter of fact, after I paid you that visit."

Marcus frowned. "You gave up? Like Elroy?"

"Oh, no!" Mollyanna said. "He made the Harvard Orchestra, that evening when I wouldn't go to his audition. You were there, remember, outside of Locke-Ober's."

Marcus looked at her suspiciously. "If you knew it was us, why didn't you remember our deal?"

"My dear, that was years before the deal. I was only seventeen." She laughed at Marcus's bewildered face. "Was I awful? I'm sorry, but I thought it meant that Elroy didn't like me anymore."

Dawn asked, "Do you ever see him nowadays?"

"Not as much as I'd like." Mollyanna laughed weakly. "It must seem ridiculous to children like you. I'm thirty-five years old, and still in love with Elroy. Nell's daughter, Liz, takes dancing lessons in the school where I play. Sometimes her uncle comes to pick her up. He says 'hello,' but that's all. Now that he plays in the Symphony, he's a busy man."

"Liz?" Dawn's face lit up. "Nell's daughter? That's my mother!"

Marcus was stunned. "She can't be."

"Remember what I told Kelly?" Dawn said excitedly. "My mother's mother was Uncle Doo's sister. And Nell is Elroy's sister, so Liz must be Mom!"

Mollyanna glanced at the china clock. "I'll have to take

144

your word for it, but it stretches the imagination. She's only five, you know. Would you like to meet her? She's dancing in *The Nutcracker* for the Christmas Eve recital, and I was supposed to be there ten minutes ago."

Madame Korulska's School of Ballet was on Morton Street, a few blocks away from Mollyanna's boardinghouse. It was announced by a pretentious gold-lettered sign on an otherwise run-down building. Dawn thought the dark recital room with its potted ferns and rows of rickety seats was dismal, but the parents acted as if they were attending an important social event.

"Thank goodness they're not dancing the whole thing!" she said, squinting in the dim light to read the program. "Excerpts, it says here. 'Dance of the Sugar Plum Fairy'—'Waltz of the Flowers'—I hope they keep it short."

"Me too," said Marcus. He slumped down in his seat and shut his eyes. "Ballet is gross!"

Dawn scanned the list of names of children who were dancing. "This is endless. It must be a huge school. Let's hope they all dance together, not one at a time. Look, here's Mom's name! I bet Nell is in the audience."

Marcus spotted her in the front row, sitting next to Elroy. Elroy looked more than ever like Uncle Doo, and Nell looked a little like their grandmother.

The curtain rose. Mollyanna thumped away at the piano. Swarms of little girls skipped around the stage with a scattering of sulky little boys. Parents applauded, and Madame Korulska herself appeared from time to time to sweep a gracious curtsey. Except for an envious glance at the girl who danced Clara, Dawn paid no attention. She sat through the entire performance biting her nails and scowling at her feet. How could she help Mollyanna?

145

Excerpts or not, the program seemed endless. Each number had its round of applause and curtain calls, and at the end there were speeches. By the time they got up from their chairs, Dawn and Marcus were so stiff that they could barely hobble to the main hall for refreshments.

"Did you like it?" Mollyanna asked, coming toward them with two cups of fruit punch.

"No," said Marcus.

"You played beautifully, though," Dawn added hastily.

It struck her that she didn't know which of the children had been her mother. "Where's Liz? Can you point her out to me?"

"Over by the stairs, with Nell." Mollyanna pointed, then blushed as she noticed Elroy.

"Come on, let's get a closer look!" Marcus said.

They edged through the crowd, coming up behind Elroy in time to hear him give his niece some musical advice.

"Dance your heart out!" he said enthusiastically. "And whatever you do, *never* let anyone tell you that music is pleasant, but only at the appropriate moment."

Liz hopped cheerfully around in her tiny pink slippers, but Nell shook her head. "Don't waste your breath. Liz won't go into the arts: She's training to be the nation's first female vice-president."

Dawn felt uneasy, as if she were snooping in her mother's closet without permission. Would that dimpled five-year-old really grow up to be the warm, comfortable Liz of 1986? Would she grow even older and become the sad Liz of 1999? She had her whole life before her, clean and open. It seemed like trespassing to see her now.

Marcus giggled nervously. "Should we tell her she's our mother?"

Dawn ignored the question. "Listen, I've got a plan. I

146

need to find Mollyanna and take her upstairs. You stay right where you are. Give us a couple of minutes, and then bring Elroy up too."

"How am I supposed to do that?" Marcus asked.

"I don't know. Just do it. Force him, if you have to. Tell him lies—who cares? This is our only chance, remember."

People were beginning to go home. There wasn't time to explain to Marcus, or even to Mollyanna. Dawn raced up the stairs with the young woman in tow and ran along the second-story hall, opening and shutting doors until she found one with a key in the lock.

"Wait here!" she said. "Please trust me and just wait."

She pushed Mollyanna through the door, shut it, and leaned against it, gasping for breath. A moment later Marcus appeared, followed reluctantly by Elroy.

"I did it," he told Dawn, "but it wasn't easy. I had to promise him a reward."

"He'll get it," Dawn said. "Good work, Marcus."

Elroy looked from one to the other. "Mollyanna was right. You *do* keep coming back."

"It's about time you noticed," said Marcus.

Elroy scratched his head. "I don't understand. How do you do it? And what do you want from me?"

"It's what we want *for* you that matters," said Dawn. "Listen, the first time you met us, we convinced you to switch that silly stereoscope for a flute, right?"

"Was that really you?" Elroy asked.

"It sure was. And the second time, we helped you to rescue a damsel in distress, and as a result, your father let you take music lessons. Admit it!"

Elroy nodded.

"Then we got rid of that pickle-brained Lillian Prendergast who thought you looked like a clown. And the last

147

time you saw us, we got you to the audition on time. Are you grateful?"

Elroy opened his mouth, but Dawn didn't give him a chance to answer. "We're your guardian angels, and we're helping you one more time. Marcus promised you a reward, didn't he?"

Stepping forward, she gestured dramatically toward the door behind her. "Inside, and greet your future!"

Marcus watched in admiration as his sister slammed the door and locked it. "What was in there?" he whispered.

"Mollyanna."

Marcus thought for a moment. "I get it. But where does the door go?"

"To the broom closet." Dawn broke into a grin.

"Hey, wait a minute!" said Marcus. "You can't do that— it's Christmas Eve! Everybody's gone!"

"Don't worry, they'll think it's romantic." Dawn started walking toward the stairs. "Are you coming home or not?"

"Coming," Marcus said, "but all the same, I call it a dirty trick."

Liz and Harry Foster looked tanned, relaxed, and cheerful. "Where have you two been? We walked in and there wasn't a soul around. Where are Uncle Doo and Aunt Anna?"

Dawn wriggled out of her father's hug. "Aunt who?"

Before he could answer, Uncle Doo himself came through the front door, followed by Miss Purvis.

Dawn stared. Uncle Doo looked different. The deep lines between his brows were gone, for one thing, and his face seemed fuller. There was nothing bitter left in it at all.

"Anna! Elroy!" Harry Foster cried. He kissed Miss Purvis on both cheeks and shook Uncle Doo's hand vigorously.

148

"How did it go? You two saved our lives, let me tell you. Liz and I feel twenty years younger."

Miss Purvis smiled. "They didn't give us a bit of trouble. I just felt sad that we never had children of our own."

"Wait a moment!" Dawn's face became stormy. "That's all wrong. How come he married you? He was supposed to marry Mollyanna!"

Miss Purvis bustled her out of the room. "Silly!" she whispered when they were alone. "Don't you know who I am? I knew who *you* were when I met you, last Friday at the concert."

Her blue eyes sparkled, and Dawn gasped. "Mollyanna! But why did you change your name?"

Miss Purvis shrugged. "I thought 'Mollyanna' was un-dignified. I wanted a real career, not just a job playing for pint-sized ballerinas in Forest Hills. I shortened my name to Anna for luck."

Dawn remembered how their last visit had ended, and blushed. "How long did you have to stay in the broom closet?"

"Hours. But when the night watchman let us out, I had Elroy's fraternity ring on my finger. We were married the next spring, and your own mother was our flower girl—little show-off! But that was forty-three years ago."

Dawn smiled. "So you've been married forty-three years, and you both got your Hearts' Desires. But what about Uncle Doo? Does he remember us?"

Miss Purvis said, "He does now, and he's a bit confused, but we promised not to ask any questions. The point is that now we're all happy."

All happy. All happy.

The words throbbed, echoed, kept time with the music as Uncle Doo and his wife of forty-three years played

149

through the movements of the Bach sonata. Uncle Doo was happy, Dawn could see, and Mollyanna had a soft glow on her face. Her parents sat shoulder to shoulder as if their week away had made them inseparable. Marcus had a dazed, expectant look on his face: a look meaning Christmas morning and stockings, that Dawn thought she would never have again. What about Dawn?

Her mother glanced at her and smiled reassuringly. Dawn smiled back, but she ached inside. Why? Hadn't she been successful and found two Hearts' Desires?

She felt empty, as if something had been stolen away from her, and no one would ever believe her or understand. Not Marcus, or her parents, or Uncle Doo and Mollyanna. She tried to tune out the music and see herself on T.V. It used to be easy, but now it was impossible. No Clara appeared to dance on an imaginary stage. No Dawn Foster enchanted the public with her singing flute.

Instead, another flute pierced through her dreams—Uncle Doo's. It lulled her, told a story, begged her to sing with it. "You can do it!" it sang. "Listen to me, pay attention. You can do it too!"

The music stopped. The minister spoke again to the congregation. Candles were lit, and there were carols. The Fosters walked home along a moonlit beach with Mollyanna and Uncle Doo. Bells chimed. It was Christmas morning. But Dawn had one thing only on her mind.

"Can I have the car keys?" she asked before they reached Uncle Doo's condominium.

Her father reached into his pocket. "Here you go. You're not planning to drive away, I hope."

"I need my flute," Dawn said. "I left it under the seat when you went to Key West, but I want it now."

150

Her father stared. "I'm sorry, Dawn," he said gently. "I don't understand. You left your what?"

"My flute. Accidentally on purpose, because I didn't want to practice. Now I do."

Her mother caught her last words. Both parents looked perplexed. "You're tired, Dawnie. You're half asleep."

"What's wrong?" Dawn asked. "Did you lose it? Did someone steal it out of the car?"

Liz Foster put her arms around her daughter. "You're not making sense, but you can explain tomorrow. Did you go to sleep and dream of flutes?"

Dawn pulled away. "What do you mean? What happened to my flute?"

"You don't have a flute, sweetheart. You never did. Are you sure you're all right?"

"I'm fine. I'm sorry. I guess you're right, I was half asleep."

Dawn thought of the lessons she had been taking for three years. She thought of the practicing. Would she have to do that all over again? And what about her flute—what had become of it?"

"Marcus!" she whispered when they had gone to bed. "Am I crazy? Did I dream it up?"

"I don't know," he said. "*I* remember, but Mom and Dad obviously don't. I bet I know what happened, though."

Dawn stared into the darkness. "What happened?"

"It's the same flute," Marcus said, rolling over and pulling the covers around him. "Remember how Mom kept saying it was almost a century old and it belonged to her great-uncle Arthur? Well, that's got to be the Arthur whose box the flute was in, until we changed boxes. So instead of being handed down to you after all these years, it went to Elroy on his tenth birthday."

151

"You know something?" said Dawn. "For a dummy, you aren't so dumb. Why didn't you tell me before?"

"I didn't think of it before. I didn't figure it out until I was bored in church tonight."

Dawn sighed. "If I never had the flute in the first place, I probably won't even remember how to play a scale. I'll have to start over, lessons and all."

The bedroom door opened and Uncle Doo appeared, silhouetted against the light of the hallway. He was wearing red-and-white striped pajamas, and his hair was rumpled. "What's all this noise? If you kids don't get to sleep, you won't wake up on time for stockings."

"It's not me, it's Dawn," Marcus said. "She's all upset because she doesn't know how to play the flute."

Uncle Doo smiled at Dawn. "You want to play the flute? Why not? If you lived a little closer, I'd teach you myself. It takes hard work, though. You have no idea how much hard work went into my career as a flutist."

Marcus giggled. "Want to bet?"

"I'll tell you what," said Uncle Doo. "Ask your parents to get you a student flute, Dawn, and start taking lessons up in Massachusetts. Then you can visit me a couple of times a year, and I'll give you some extra coaching."

"A couple of times a year?" Dawn repeated. She felt dazed.

"That's right. I told your parents you were welcome anytime you wanted to come down, both of you. Our house is your house. But at this hour of the night, it's for sleeping in, if you don't mind."

After Uncle Doo had shut the door again, Dawn sat bolt upright in her bed. "Coaching? The nerve of him! A week ago he didn't know how to play at all, and now he says *he'll* teach *me*!"

Marcus was already half asleep. "Why bother?" he mumbled. "When you had the flute you never practiced anyway, so who cares?"

For a moment there was silence. "I care," said Dawn.